"The Earth has a Remarkable Ability to Heal Itself"

BOOKS BY DONALD T. PHILLIPS

Jesus

AND

Climate Change

A Parable of the Earth

DONALD T PHILLIPS

Written and Published by Donald T. Phillips

"The Earth has a Remarkable Ability to Heal Itself"

<u>Credits</u>: *Cover Image: "NASA's Earth Observatory," 2010; "NASA Know Your Earth Project." Hand salute: Author photo.*

ISBN: 978-0-9828484-3-2

Jesus

and

Climate Change

A Parable of the Earth

He was born in a poor neighborhood of Mexico City and was christened Jesus Garcia Gomez. His mother was a devout Catholic who read the Bible to him every day. Six weeks after his little sister was born, she began suffering from colic and would scream in agony for several hours every night at dinnertime. One evening, he walked over and put his hand on her tummy. The tension in the baby's body relaxed and her high-pitched shrieks stopped. From then on, whenever the crying was particularly bad, his mother would call him over and, almost always, the baby became calm. He did not speak until the age of three, his large ocean eyes taking in everything around him. Then one day, he began talking in full sentences. When he was four years old, his parents took him to visit the Basilica de Guadalupe during the height of the yearly pilgrimage. But while on the square in the middle of the crowd, he wandered away from his family. After a frantic search, his father found him sitting in a front pew in the Basilica staring up at the image of the Virgin on the cloak. The mid-afternoon sun shining through the translucent glass ceiling produced enchanting angled rays of light above the altar.

Sitting down next to Jesus, his father asked, "What are you doing, son?"

"Listening," came the reply.

When the boy was five, his family moved to the United States in search of a better life. They settled in a densely populated Southern California barrio on the western edge the Los Angeles River. On their side of the canal, houses were worth a pittance. On the other side, at least ten-to-twenty times more. It was here that Jesus grew from childhood to adolescence. His father worked whatever day jobs he could find. His mother was always at home caring for the children. The boy never lied to his mother, never evaded, never turned a corner to avoid any responsibility. He dutifully attended church and eventually taught Sunday school to the younger kids. The parish priest was astonished both at the youngster's knowledge of scripture and that he often wanted to discuss the Sunday sermon.

The walk from his home to the church was along tough neighborhood streets where gangs were rampant. At first, Jesus was harassed. But after awhile, the gangs left him alone, in part, because he was so amiable and good-natured. He made friends with most of the other kids in the barrio by earning their trust and respect. Jesus was, in fact, often the peacemaker, stepping in and breaking up fights sometimes by telling one or both sides to "temper their anger" or "turn the other cheek."

At church one day, Jesus met a visiting priest from another diocese who had a kind of "healing" ability. "I can feel energy emanating from my palms," he said. "I think it's some sort of magnetic field. Here, let me touch your arm. Do you feel it?"

"Yes, I do," replied Jesus, who sensed warmth and what seemed like a swirling motion.

"I'm extremely sensitive to touch," continued the priest, "and am sometimes able to help people who have minor aches and pains – just by placing my hands on them. Their area of discomfort feels to me like a cloud of heavy air."

"You know, I think I may have something like that, Father," said Jesus.

"Oh?"

"Yes, since I was very young."

"Put your hands on the back of my neck," said the priest. "It's been stiff lately."

When Jesus did so, the priest said, "Hmm, you may, indeed, have a gift, young man."

"What should I do?"

"Well, I'd try it out a few times, but only with family and close friends. Be cautious and discreet. If it works even once in awhile, people may spread rumors that you are some kind of faith healer – and that would cause you problems."

"What if it works?"

"Then you are blessed and must use your natural talent wisely. You'll be able to tell soon enough."

The priest walked away feeling the back of his neck, wondering if it felt better.

Jesus was immediately intrigued that an invisible force like a magnetic field might explain the priest's hands-on healing. The young man not only loved science, but was curious about almost everything. This love of learning was the catalyst for an almost flawless scholastic record in high school, which earned him a full academic scholarship to the University of Southern California. It was there that he studied the four major branches of the earth sciences: geology, meteorology, oceanography, and astronomy.

As an undergraduate, Jesus also took extra classes on a variety of subjects not required for his degree, such as history, philosophy, and even the odd course on science fiction. He often could be found reading Shakespeare, Cervantes, and the romantic poets in his spare time. Those books were kept in the backpack he always wore when riding his bike around campus, and when he walked, it was perpetually slung over his left shoulder.

After earning his Bachelor of Science degree, Jesus went on to Stanford for a Master's where he studied the science of geology in detail. Classroom study for him was motivating, but he particularly loved being outdoors on field trips, where he often wandered away from the group to explore on his own.

"Where is Garcia now?" an annoyed professor once asked.

"See those hawks over there?" said a student. "He's on that bluff watching them circle. He likes to be up high to see the big picture."

"Well, go get him, will you. It's time to move on."

The student started up the mountain, climbing through the brush, around the boulders, and between the trees. He finally found Jesus sitting on the overlook reading a thin paperback.

"There you are!" said the student. "Christ, the wind up here really cuts through you, doesn't it?"

"Here, put this on," said Jesus, pulling a jacket out of his backpack. "I'm not cold."

"Hey, Doc says it's time to go."

"Look at those sunbeams shining through the clouds, will you."

"Yeah, I see them."

"Hey, listen to this," said Jesus reading from his book:

There's a certain Slant of light,
Winter Afternoons –
That oppresses, like the Heft
Of Cathedral Tunes –

Heavenly Hurt, it gives us –
We can find no scar,
But internal difference,
Where the Meanings, are –

None may teach it – Any –
'Tis the Seal Despair –
An imperial affliction
Sent us of the Air –

When it comes, the Landscape listens –
Shadows – hold their breath –
When it goes, 'tis like the Distance
On the look of Death.

"Emily Dickinson," Jesus concluded.

"Gee, that's really beautiful, buddy. But we better get going or we'll receive the look of death from our prof. C'mon!"

By now, Jesus had grown to a lean six feet in height. He was strong physically, clean-shaven, with long dark brown hair that he often wore in a ponytail. He was universally liked and a good friend to those around him.

After completing his degree at Stanford with a master's thesis documenting glaciers in North America, Jesus went on to Harvard where he earned a PhD in geology. His dissertation proposed a new process for sequestration of carbon dioxide in oil and gas operations. Although many of his friends and professors urged him to enter academia at a major university, Jesus decided to go into the energy industry where, as he told a friend, "help is needed." And despite now having earned a doctorate from a prestigious university, he vowed never to use the title "Dr." in front of his name.

"Look at this kid's resume," said a human resources manager for Global Energy Incorporated to his colleagues. "USC Bachelors, Stanford Masters, PhD from Harvard. Straight A's across the board."

"Wow! Where's he from?"

"Grew up in Los Angeles. He's a minority, too."

"Well, we certainly could use one of them."

"He studied glacier's in the U.S. and Canada at Stanford – carbon sequestration at Harvard."

"Oh, no. He's not one of those global warming guys, is he?"

"Won't matter, I think. Even if he is, we can say we've hired people to look at the issue."

"Where would we put him? R&D, maybe?"

"Sounds like the creative kind. Could start him out in exploration. See how he does."

"Okay, we better fly him down here for an interview before somebody else picks him up."

A month later, Jesus walked into Global Energy's main headquarters as a new employee. "Welcome to Houston, Jesus," said the HR representative. "Is that how you pronounce your name?"

"Thank you," he replied with a smile. "I'm Hay-Soos."

"Oh, I'm sorry."

"That's okay. Happens all the time."

"Well, let me give you a tour of the building and then we'll introduce you to people in your department."

The woman led Jesus down a long hall of offices that led out into a small atrium in front of the auditorium where she paused in front of a beautiful mahogany wall table under a large oil painting. "This is a portrait of our founder, who recently passed away at the age of 98," she said. "The lace linen on the table is made from Byssus, an extremely rare sea silk native to the Mediterranean Sea. This particular piece is one of the largest in the world. The candles are hand crafted in France and the vessels are made of gold leaf. We light them every morning and keep them burning all day. It's a sort of eternal flame. He was a great man."

"I'm sure he was," said Jesus. "Very impressive."

"We chose this place to memorialize him, because the midafternoon sunlight illuminates the atrium. You should drop by this afternoon and see it."

"I will."

"Here's our auditorium," she continued, walking to her right. "It seats 1,000 and we use it for special events and major presentations to our employees.

"Now, let's go upstairs and walk through the exploration department. We'll also stop to see your boss, Nick, to say hi. He'll want to take you to lunch after you sign all your papers."

People at Global Energy found Jesus to be a quiet, hard-working employee. He was always on time, always in his office at his drafting table – and he was courteous and respectful to everyone. One thing some found odd, however, is that he rarely, if ever, went to lunch with his colleagues, which was an accepted way of building relationships and making friends. Jesus, rather, usually struck out on his own during the lunch break.

He began by walking around downtown close to Global's office building. Then he got on his bicycle and headed west, because that's where human resources suggested he look for a place to live. Just outside of downtown, he encountered an area of unconventional restaurants and bars interspersed with apartments, townhomes, and small single-family houses. But he was soon pedaling through a wealthy neighborhood replete with beautifully landscaped lawns, carriage houses, verandas, and a country club with a championship golf course. On trash days, the bins overflowed with food still good enough to eat – and Jesus could only smile as he rode by the opulent mansions with their brick exteriors, patterned roofs, and swimming pools. "Tombs for the super wealthy," he thought to himself.

On another day, Jesus headed east from downtown where he rode by several large parks, a professional sports stadium, and a number of industrial sites. Farther east, beyond the major north-south interstate highway running through the center of Houston, he found himself rolling through streets with run down houses, unkempt lawns, and dead or dying trees. Homeless people could be seen wandering around at street intersections, some picking through trash dumpsters, some pushing shopping carts filled with all their belongings. With a quick turn to the north, Jesus biked right up to the banks of Buffalo Bayou, Greater Houston's heavily urbanized river, which reminded him of the LA River and his boyhood home.

On his way back to the office, Jesus spotted Our Lady of Guadalupe Catholic Church. Immediately drawn to it, he parked his bike outside, went into the chapel, and sat in the first pew. The church was simple and unadorned, and he could not stop staring at the grand image of the Virgin of Guadalupe hanging behind the altar. After about ten minutes, the parish priest walked over and sat down next to him. "Beautiful, isn't it," he said.

Jesus nodded.

"The story goes that, in 1531, the Blessed Virgin appeared before a peasant named Juan Diego in Mexico and transformed a handful of roses into this image on the interior of his Aztec cloak. Several healing miracles have been attributed to it. Of course, the original is at the Basilica in Mexico City."

"Yes, I've seen it."

The priest paused a moment and then extended his hand. "I'm Miguel."

"Jesus Garcia, Father," he replied, accepting the handshake. "I'm new here."

"Welcome, then. Our parish was founded in 1912 and was the first church in Houston to offer services in Spanish. We are one of the poorest Catholic churches in the United States."

"Oh?" said Jesus.

"Yes, the majority of our parishioners are from Mexico and Central America, or are descended from immigrants. Most work in low-wage jobs and struggle to make ends meet. We serve a great many unemployed and homeless people."

"I see."

"May I ask what brought you to our city?"

"Yes, Father. I just took a job in the energy industry. I'm on my lunch break . . . . Oh, I need to be getting back."

As the two walked back to the main entrance, Father Miguel asked if there was anything he could do for Jesus.

"Well, I need a place to stay," he answered. "Nothing fancy."

"We'll see what we can find."

As they walked outside, Jesus looked around and smiled. "My bike is gone," he said."

"Oh, my goodness. We'll get it back for you."

"It's okay. Whoever took it probably needs it. I can get another."

"Come. My car's right over here," said the priest. "I'll drive you back to your office."

Six months after joining the company, Jesus submitted his work in the area he was assigned, East Texas. A major oil and gas producing area that was already heavily explored, most companies shied away from exploration. Even Global Energy limited its activity to existing production. But the young geologist's job was to find new undiscovered fields. Everybody realized he had a difficult task, in part, because the area had been producing since 1930. Its mammoth East Texas Field had supplied three-quarters of all the oil to the Allied forces during World War II. So the conventional view was that there was really nothing left to be found. For his work, however, Jesus used a creative approach to exploration by doing a vast regional study of all the existing oil and gas fields, determining the key geologic features they had in common, and then mapping those features over the entire area. Then, by projecting in between the existing fields, he was able to generate a dozen new prospects.

"Holy mackerel," said his boss, Nick, when he first saw the work. "Look at that! Where did you come up with the idea to do it this way?"

"Just seemed natural," Jesus replied.

"Well, the prospects really pop out on your maps! It's amazing!"

All of a sudden, Jesus's profile was on the rise at Global. With his work, he was attracting attention not only from the executives, but also from people in his own department, some of whom were jealous.

"Boy, the executives are really gullible, aren't they?" said one geologist. "Generating so many prospects in an area that's already been heavily drilled? Who does he think he's kidding?"

"He dresses kind of shabby, too, don't you think?" said another.

"Yeah, those khaki pants that are always frayed at the cuffs. And those worn shoes."

"How come he won't go to lunch with any of us?"

"Yeah, we ask him all the time."

"But he goes out every day at lunch."

"Where does he go?"

"He never brings a sack lunch, so he must eat somewhere."

"Well, then why doesn't he eat with us once in a while?"

"I wonder what he's doing."

"Why don't we follow him one day and see?"

"Good idea. But we'll need a bike. He rides every day."

"I can bring one in."

"Me, too."

"Let's do it."

The next day, two of the geologists brought in their bicycles and followed Jesus during his lunch break, keeping a safe distance so as not to be noticed. Upon arriving back at the office, they went down to the coffee room and met with the others.

"What happened?" they all wanted to know. "Where did he go?"

"Well, he walked his bike out to the hot dog stand across the street and started talking in Spanish to the vendor like they were old buddies. Then he ate the hot dog while he rode east. A whole bunch of people waved at him and said hi as he passed."

"Really? How could he know so many people already?"

"Well, it seemed like nearly everybody did. And get this, when he waved back, he used the Vulcan hand salute."

"What's that?"

"C'mon, you know – from Star Trek."

"Huh?"

"You hold up your hand like this, with the ring and center fingers slightly separated – and say "Live long and prosper."

"That's really weird, man! Why would he do that?"

"I don't know. He must be a Trekkie."

"Never mind that. What happened next?"

"Well, he headed straight to the Catholic Church in the Second Ward, rode around back, and went inside. I peered through a window and saw him in a line serving food to poor people. After about half an hour, he got on his bike and pedaled over to a little shack of a house, went inside, and came out five minutes later with a new shirt on. I think he had spilled some rice or beans or something on the old one. Then he headed back to the office and actually got here on time."

"That's it?"

"Yep, that's it."

Everybody just shrugged and went back to their offices.

One year later a Category 4 hurricane struck Houston and the surrounding Gulf coast. The storm had sustained winds of 150 miles per hour, and it stalled for three days dumping five feet of rain on the city. Almost all mobile trailers were severely damaged, fifty percent of houses had their roofs blown off, large trees were entirely uprooted or snapped in half at the trunks, and windows on high rise buildings were blown out. So many homes were rendered uninhabitable that 40,000 people were forced into public shelters. Catastrophic flooding during the first 24 hours resulted in many more thousands of people having to be rescued, usually by average citizens who happened to be on the spot.

On that first day, Jesus awoke to a foot of water in his rental house. He immediately rose and headed over to the church where he was certain people would congregate for help. On the way, he saw a car stranded in the middle of the road and people making a human chain to get to the occupants through the rushing torrent. Jesus joined the chain and the group was successful in pulling out a woman and her six-year-old son. But once on the side of the road, the woman began screaming that her younger daughter was still in the back seat.

"Quick, let's make the chain, again," someone yelled.

"No time," said Jesus, who thrust himself into the water and rushed out to the almost completely submerged vehicle. Diving out of sight, he emerged a few moments later holding the limp unconscious child. After hurrying back, Jesus began mouth-to-mouth resuscitation on the little girl. He performed four strong breaths, then checked for a pulse, but found none. He repeated the cycle a couple of more times, but to no avail. As the anxious mother and other rescuers looked on, Jesus placed his hands over the child's heart, leaned down and whispered something in her ear. Then he began mouth-to-mouth again. Suddenly, the girl started spitting up water and took a couple of deep breaths. "Mama!" she cried. "Mama!"

"She'll be okay," said Jesus, who got up and immediately sprinted off toward the church.

"Wait," said one of the onlookers. "Who are you? . . . . Thank you!"

"Did you all see that?" said another person. "Was it my imagination or did the current lessen when he went back out to the car?"

"Yes, it did!" said a woman. "I saw it!"

When Jesus reached the church, he found hundreds of people seeking shelter. The clergy and quick-responding volunteers did what they could to calm everybody. Blankets, food, and water were provided, and prayers were offered. Over the next couple of weeks, Our Lady of Guadalupe led relief efforts in the community, including coordinating with the Salvation Army, the Red Cross, and FEMA. With his own home flooded, Jesus simply stayed at the church and joined the hundreds of other volunteers.

As the waters finally receded, people all across Houston ventured out to survey the damage. A quarter of a million people were without power. More than a thousand homes had been destroyed. Fifteen hundred public buildings, hotels, and churches now housed victims of the storm, many of whom were destined to remain homeless for months. One-third of the nation's fourth largest city had quite literally been underwater. The National Weather Service called it a 1,000-year flood and further stated that, as the hurricane passed over the Texas and Louisiana gulf coasts, it had spawned the largest rainfall event in United States history.

Over the next several days, Jesus bicycled through his neighborhood helping people where he could. One afternoon, he recognized one of the employees from his office.

"Rodrigo!" he said, laying down his bike and walking up. "Cómo estás?"

"Hola," replied Rodrigo with a smile. "Bien, bien."

"You're fixing up your mobile home?" Jesus asked, continuing the conversation in Spanish.

"Yes. We built it up eight feet, but we still had four feet of water in it when the flood came."

"Rodrigo, black mold is setting into the walls," said Jesus, as the two walked through the trailer. "There's no way you can salvage this unless you take out all of the wood frame and replace it."

"I can't afford to do that."

"Well, the government has money to help."

"I am undocumented, so I can't apply. And I have two DACA children in college who I don't want to put at risk."

Jesus paused for a moment. "Okay, my friend," he said. "I'll buy all the wood and we'll rebuild it from the ground up."

"Oh no, it'll cost too much."

"It's okay. I have enough money to help you with this. We'll do it together."

When Rodrigo began to cry, Jesus embraced him. "Remember, my friend," he said. *"We are pressed on every side by troubles, but we are not crushed and broken."*

Not long after Global Energy's storm-suspended operations resumed, one of the East Texas prospects Jesus had generated was drilled and judged a major discovery. In fact, it was the biggest domestic gas discovery for the company in five years. As a result, Jesus was promoted to senior exploration geologist, given a bonus, and moved to an office with a window. He immediately cashed the bonus check and gave half the money to Father Miguel, 25 percent to the American Red Cross, and used the rest to help his neighbors with their ongoing recoveries from the storm.

After this devastating hurricane, Jesus decided to take a more detailed look at the latest science behind climate change. Every night for the next month, he immersed himself in the most recent United Nations and United States Government reports. He also read many of the scientific papers upon which those reports were based in order to determine whether or not the research conducted was solid. And after concluding his research, Jesus was alarmed. "My God," he said to himself. "This could mean the end of the world as we know it." Fires, floods, droughts, searing temperatures, scarcity of food and water, disease, and mass migrations were all likely coming. And many people would view it as nothing less than an Armageddon.

Now that he understood the full truth, Jesus began talking to his fellow employees about climate change. But rather than sound a panic, he started slowly and deliberately by having personal conversations with individuals.

There were five irrefutable scientific lines of evidence that proved climate change was real, he told people:

1) Ice is melting all over the world, including the Arctic, Antarctic, Greenland, and glaciers everywhere.

2) The earth is hotter now than in the past and average global temperatures continue to rise.

3) Ocean surface water temperatures have increased everywhere.

4) Global mean seal level has risen and continues to rise.

5) Carbon dioxide (CO_2) levels in the earth's atmosphere have skyrocketed to levels never before seen in human history.

Pretty soon there was a buzz going around the office about this likeable geologist speaking openly about climate change. Most of the talk was met with skepticism and even outrage. After all, this was a subject that was basically taboo, even sacrilege, in an energy company. Employees only whispered about it behind closed doors. Fossil fuels like oil, gas, and coal couldn't possibly be to blame for global warming. Or could they? What would that mean for the industry? Even more important, what would it mean for our jobs? Our livelihoods? Our children? Best not to talk about it. Not even a little bit.

On the other hand, a strong internal minority rejected the idea of simply ignoring climate change. "It's like burying your head in the sand to avoid facing the truth," some said. These people were glad someone had finally mustered the courage to speak openly about the issue. And wanting to know more, they actually encouraged Jesus to hold an assembly for all employees. "Okay," he responded. "If you set it up, I'll be there."

A week later, Jesus led a discussion on climate change in the company's auditorium. Some people came out of curiosity to hear what was going to be said. Some came out of a sincere interest in a problem that most in the industry had been ignoring. Interestingly enough, a large contingent of service-level employees showed up, because word had gotten around about the help Jesus had given Rodrigo – although not from Jesus, himself. "We don't do our good deeds publicly or to be admired," he had told his friend.

After beginning with the five irrefutable lines of evidence, Jesus spoke about the storm that hit Houston and why it had been made worse by climate change. "We already know that warm water is the main energy source in a hurricane," he said. "That's why hurricane season peaks in the summer. As the storm moves along, heat is pulled up from the water and transformed into wind energy. Well, because of climate change, seawater is hotter and there is more moisture in the air, which helps the hurricane grow larger and last longer.

"That's what happened to us," he continued. "Rainfall in this storm was 38 percent higher than anything we've ever before experienced. And we've never had a hurricane last this long. They usually blow right through in a matter of hours. This one stalled over our city for three days which, of course, caused such damage that it will take us years to fully recover. Now, I know you've heard this before, but the storm caused $125 billion in damage. More than 100 people died. A million motor vehicles were destroyed, 250,000 homes were damaged, and on and on and on.

"One thing we also know is that the storm did not discriminate. East or west, rich or poor – all over the city, everybody got hit hard. Many middle class homes had three feet of water in their upstairs floors. In some areas 95 percent of all the houses were flooded. One wealthy retirement community on the west side of town looked like a war zone after the hurricane went through. Most of the people who live there are in their 80s and are choosing not to rebuild, although they probably have the means to do so. So just imagine what it's like for those who live in more modest housing, who have little savings in the bank, who have no flood insurance, and who cannot turn to the government for help. What do they do? Where do they go? It's very clear to me, and I hope it's obvious to all of us, that people with the least are hurt the most by these ever-worsening storms.

"And the ironic thing is that we humans have done it to ourselves! *That* is a scientific fact!

"We also have not been good shepherds of the earth. And *that* is a *spiritual* truth."

As soon as the audience realized that Jesus had finished his opening remarks, a hand in the front row went up. "Excuse me," said the employee, "I'm not sure I believe a word of anything you just said. But with that understood, let me ask you this: Haven't there been times in history where the climate has changed? A lot of people say we're just going through another natural cycle – and that there is no real proof it's being caused by human activity."

Jesus answered directly. "Yes, the climate has fluctuated throughout the earth's past. There have been, for example, five major ice ages in geologic history. Each lasted many millions of years. In fact, we're in one now, which is why we have ice at the north and south poles. This ice age started a little less then 3 million years ago and has produced quite a few mini-ice ages that come and go about every 40 to 100 thousand years. Glaciers advance and then they recede. They grow and they melt. And these fluctuations are obviously caused by global temperatures going up and then going down.

"Now let me get to the second part of your question. Yes, there is proof that we're causing it.

"During these smaller ice ages, over the last 700,000 years or so, carbon dioxide levels in the atmosphere ranged from 170 to 280 parts per million. But CO2 in the atmosphere right now is more than 400 ppm and headed higher. In fact, the highest concentration of CO2 in all of geologic time prior to the early 20th century was only 300. And, of course, that's about the time the modern industrial revolution began and we first started using fossil fuels on a massive scale. So, in about 100 years, we've added more than 100 parts per million of carbon dioxide to the earth's atmosphere. And that is alarmingly fast – especially in terms of geologic time where we're used to dealing with millions of years for such significant changes to occur.

"Clearly, natural changes in the earth simply cannot explain such a dramatic increase," continued Jesus. "So that is circumstantial evidence that human beings are causing climate change. But the hard proof comes from analyzing in detail the carbon dioxide in the air. Carbon from fossil fuels, like oil, gas, or coal, has a specific identifier – kind of like a fingerprint – and we can measure it compared to carbon from other sources. Scientists have done it successfully and the results are undeniable. Our use of fossil fuels has driven CO2 levels in the atmosphere up to previously unimaginable levels and that, in turn, has caused the climate change we're seeing today."

"So, there is proof that human activity is causing the earth to get hotter. And the earth is *definitely* getting hotter. Scientists, in fact, have routinely measured some of the highest temperatures ever recorded on our planet. Nearly every year, we hear that we just experienced the hottest year on record, or the hottest month on record, or the hottest decade. We're seeing temperatures over 100 degrees in Japan, 110 degrees in Arizona, 120 in the Middle East, 130 in India. Prolonged heat waves are becoming the rule rather than the exception. As a result, heat-related deaths are on the rise nearly everywhere.

After a long pause, another hand in the audience went up. "Is there time to fix this? Or is it too late?"

"Well, I personally believe that yes, there is time to reverse the trend and no, it's not too late. The earth has a remarkable ability to heal itself. But we must help it along. And we must start taking action now.

"Hey, our time is almost up and I know we all have to be getting back to work," said Jesus. "How about one more question? Yes."

"I'm a Christian and my faith teaches me that a higher power has control over something like this and that we shouldn't be worried about it."

"Yes, I understand," Jesus replied. "But I like what John F. Kennedy said in his inaugural address. 'Here on earth, God's work must truly be our own.'"

Word of the meeting spread like wildfire around Global's workplace and employees almost immediately broke into two groups. The larger group consisted of hardcore climate change deniers who were angry at Jesus for even suggesting that their industry had anything to do with the causes of global warming. Some mid-level women felt particularly threatened that they might lose their jobs, their privileged lifestyles, and their comfortable status quo. The more they talked among themselves – and talk they did, with whispers behind closed doors – the more angry they became at Jesus. This large group also included higher-level male executives who savored their stock options and yearly bonus checks. And clearly they believed that the "ranting of this young agitator" could impact future earnings."

The smaller group was mostly silent, fearful of speaking out. But a few professionals who knew the truth behind the science approached Jesus quietly and offered their support. There were three geologists, three geophysicists, two engineers, and a geochemist who got together with Jesus in the mornings prior to work to discuss the way forward.

"There was so much more that could have been discussed in that meeting," said Pete, one of the engineers. "Global temperatures, warming oceans, decreased snow cover, extreme weather events, ocean acidification, flooding in Florida coastal cities during the day when the sun is shining."

"Yes, we have to get the word out fast," said the geochemist.

"Well, I agree," said Jesus. "But we didn't have much time at that first meeting. And we can't be too technical or we'll lose people. Eyes will glaze over and they'll stop listening. We have to present the truth to them in an interesting way. We also have to change the minds of people who have an innate bias and a dogmatic view. When people's hearts become calloused by wealth and greed, they lose their ability to see and hear at deeper levels – and often abandon their integrity. So we cannot persuade them overnight. It'll take time and a persistent effort. Fortunately, that's one thing we have on our side – time – at least from a human perspective."

"But, in geologic time, it's happening so fast," said Madeleine, one of the geologists.

"Well, look at it this way. The seas will not rise five feet in an instant. They'll rise gradually and it will last decades. So I think we should take a more long-term view to prepare our message. Let's not rush. Let's have the facts on our side. If we shoot from the hip and answer questions incorrectly, we'll be attacked and our mission will be set back. 'Gradual' is the key word here. 'Gradual' sea level rise. 'Gradual' change. And as the poet said, 'The truth must dazzle gradually or every man be blind.'"

"Okay, okay," said a geophysicist. "But we've got to counter these anti-climate change people in the office."

"Yes," said an engineer. "They're already whispering behind our backs, saying all kinds of terrible things about us. They hate us."

"Well, maybe," said Jesus. "But we can't hate them back. We have to try to win them over. And we can't do that with anger or animosity. It'll shut them right down. I really believe we have to speak to both sides with courtesy, respect, and above all – with scientific facts – which is the closest we can get to truth about the physical world."

"Agreed," said Pete. "But the extreme hatred coming from some of these people is awful. It's almost like there are two sides here, one good and one evil."

"I wouldn't exactly characterize their behavior as evil. And, personally, I try to be very careful when using that word, because people view it in different ways. Although there is true evil in the world, and it needs to be discussed, I think selfish and unselfish personalities are more common to human beings. That's how we evolved as a species. And with time, it has led to the haves and the have-nots, the rich and the poor, people who have food to waste and people who can barely afford to eat – or can't afford to eat at all."

After talking for about a half hour, the group was heading back to work when Jesus mentioned that he had to drive up to East Texas to sit one of his wildcat wells and would be out of pocket for a week to ten days.

"Hope it hits," said Madeleine.

A couple of weeks later, Jesus was taking a shortcut to work through some back alleys when he was stopped by a man with a gun who demanded his wallet.

"Here," said Jesus. "You can have it all."

Jesus then began speaking to the man, quietly and kindly, in Spanish. Pretty soon, the man lowered his gun and began to cry. He needed the money, he said, to feed his family. He'd never done anything like this before, but he was desperate. Then he apologized and handed the wallet back.

"Thank you, Juan," said Jesus. "Here, you keep the cash and I'll keep the rest. Come see us this Sunday at Our Lady of Guadalupe."

"Si, Señor," replied Juan, wiping his tears away. "Gracias, amigo. Muchas gracias."

Jesus then got back on his bike and pedaled as fast as he could to the office. As he was walking through the lobby, an administration employee named Jesse was talking to one of the security guards, who looked up.

"Jesus, don't you ever sweat?" asked the guard. "This is one of the hottest, muggiest days I've ever seen in Houston. And you just get off your bike without a bead of perspiration on you, looking like you're headed to a first date with a beautiful woman."

"Oh, I'm cool, Charles," he replied with a smile. "What are you two guys up to?"

"Well, somebody stole Jesse's bike and we were just writing it up."

"What? Right out of the office upstairs?" asked Jesus.

"No, I just left it here in the lobby for a few minutes and when I came back down, it was gone."

"And nobody saw nothing!" said Charles.

"Wouldn't you know it," said Jesse. "And just when I was beginning to believe."

"Believe what?" asked Charles.

"Believe in bicycles. No filling up at the gas station, less expensive to buy, more exercise, more fun."

"And it's green energy," said Jesus.

"Yeah, well, I'm just depressed about the whole thing."

"Here, Jesse, take mine," said Jesus, motioning toward his own bicycle.

"Oh, no, I couldn't do that."

"Well, you need some way to get home tonight. I was going to buy a new one, anyway."

While Jesse protested, the two got on the elevator and headed back upstairs. "It's okay, Jesse," said Jesus as the doors closed. "Let me be generous."

When Jesus got off the elevator, he ran into Nick, who motioned for him to come down to his office. "Hey, kid," he said. "We just ran a production test on your second well and it's another discovery. Big one, too."

"Good. Guess I earned my paycheck today," replied Jesus.

"More than that, young man," said Nick putting an envelope into his hand. "Here's a bonus. Oh, and you've been promoted to supervisor. We want you to teach the others your regional technique. You also get a bigger office – and this one has much nicer furniture."

Smiling, Jesus simply said, "Thank you."

"Well, don't get too excited," Nick chuckled. "You still report to me."

As the two walked down to the new office, Jesus asked Nick if he had heard about the tornado that struck East Texas near the well. "Oh, yes, it was awful," said Nick. "But we were lucky. The site didn't get hit and operations weren't effected."

"Well, I met some people up there whose homes were damaged. Would it be all right if I took Friday off and drove up this weekend to help?"

"Of course, kid. Go ahead."

"Great. And thanks for the bonus check, Nick. It'll come in handy."

Every Thursday during the lunch hour, six or seven middle-aged women got together to knit, sip soda, and nibble on tea sandwiches. But mostly what they did was gossip, which is why, internal to the company, they were dubbed the "sewing circle."

"Did you hear that they promoted Jesus Garcia?" asked Lily.

"What! Why?" said Sybil and Bertha, almost in unison.

"He had another discovery."

"Well, that's good, isn't it?" asked Patty.

"Hmff," grumbled Lily. "Half of the scientists now report to him."

"How do they feel about that?" asked Aline.

"Oh, most of them are mad that he's their boss. He's just a kid for crying out loud. It's bad enough him spewing all this nonsense about global warming, now they go and promote him."

"Global warming is a hoax!"

"It sure is."

"There's something wrong with that boy," said Lily.

"Like what?" asked Patty.

"He's too quiet for one thing. I don't trust people who are too quiet. He's also too polite. Always smiling when the bosses are around. So goody goody. Most people who are that nice all the time are not really like that."

"He's got them snowed all right."

"Well, I don't know about that," Patty chirped in. "Jesus smiles all the time, not just when the executives are around. And I don't think there's anything wrong with being polite."

The women continued their knitting – almost never looking up when the others were speaking.

"I find him to be kind of a quiet soul, a kind person," said Aline, coming to Patty's defense.

"Hmff," snorted Lily. "You would."

"And there's also something soft about him. Did you notice how he never complains about anyone – or anything, for that matter."

"Never trust anybody who never complains! It's not normal!"

"Really!" agreed Bertha.

"And he never swears, never talks negatively about anybody!" continued Lily. "I tell you, there's something wrong with that boy."

Now Patty looked up. "You know what," she said, "I don't think climate change is a hoax. I talked to Jesus the other day and he took the time to show me the evidence in more detail than he did in his presentation."

"You went to that presentation?" said an annoyed Lily. "And why would you waste your time talking to that guy?"

"It's not a waste of time. Besides, how are you ever going to know what you're talking about if you don't at least study the issue and talk to him personally?"

"Hmff. And another thing! Who gave him permission to use our auditorium?"

"I'm sure he signed up to use it just like we all can," said Patty.

"Well, climate change is certainly not something our company supports!" said Sybil.

"He's also suggesting a gradual switch to renewable energies like wind and solar. And I think that's a good idea."

"He's going to put the oil and gas industry out of business," said Lily.

"Nonsense," said Patty. "Certainly not anytime soon. You should read up on climate change. We all should."

"I watch the news! I know!" said Lily.

"I think you watch that propaganda channel too much."

"Actually, I watch it all the time," said Lily. "It's right on the money, not fake."

"Personally, watching it gives me comfort," said Sybil.

"Me, too," said Bertha.

The next day, Jesus was sitting at his desk just before quitting time. "Knock, knock," said the smiling woman standing at the door. "Hi. Can I come in for a minute." She was about 5 feet four inches tall, shaped like a pear, and dressed in a professional-looking pants suit. Her hair was a wiry jet black and parted on the right side where the gray roots betrayed her upper middle age.

"Hello, Lilith," replied Jesus.

"Oh, I didn't know you knew my name."

"Of course, I do."

"Actually, I go by Lily."

"Okay. Please sit down, Lily."

"Well, so many people have been saying so many nice things about you that I wanted to come and meet you for myself."

"Very kind of you."

"You know, I'm a bit of a climate change skeptic," said Lily, again smiling broadly. "But you really believe in it, don't you?"

"Oh, yes," said Jesus. "The science behind it is solid."

"I'm sorry that I didn't make your talk in the auditorium. I was quite busy that day."

"Well, we had a pretty good turnout. Actually, there were more people there than I thought would show up."

"I've heard that you're suggesting we switch to renewable energies like wind and solar. Is that true?"

"Yes. That's where the world is headed, I believe."

"Do you think it will harm our company?"

"Not in the long term. In fact, we could be a leader in the transition. Who better than an international energy corporation?"

Lily then started to peruse the office like a nosy neighbor who wanted to see what the new owner's house looked like. She spotted several books on the credenza behind the desk, which included the latest UN and US reports on climate change, Darwin's *Origin of the Species,* and the Bible. "Oh, you have a copy of the Good Book, I see," she said.

"Yes, it's always with me," he replied.

"Those others are a little incompatible with it, don't you think?" she said, again with a broad smile.

"I was raised Catholic and I don't see any problem."

"But religion and science are like oil and water. They just don't mix."

"You know," said Jesus, "I find it interesting how both the Bible and Darwin extol inclusion and diversity. *'All people on earth will be blessed.'* *'There is neither Jew nor Greek, slave nor free, male nor female, for we are all one.'* *'Love thy neighbor.'* And Darwin concluded that diversity in the gene pool ensures success and survivability, that productivity increases with diversity, and that diversity, itself, is beautiful."

"Do you agree with the theory of evolution, Jesus?"

"Yes, I do. Actually, evolution is not a theory anymore. It's a fact."

Lily's eyes darkened for a moment and the back of her neck flushed. But she caught herself getting angry and quickly smiled. "Well, it's almost time to catch my car pool," she said, rising from her chair. "Thank you for talking to me. You're very kind. Let me know if there's anything I can do to help you."

After she left, Jesus turned his chair and looked out the window. "Oh most pernicious woman," he whispered to himself, "one may smile and smile and be a villain."

On the way home that evening, Jesus spotted an elderly woman who was working in her front yard suddenly drop her gardening tool and grimace in pain. He quickly pulled his bike over and walked up to her. "Mrs. Romero, are you all right?" he asked.

"Oh, it's this arthritis in my hands."

"Here, let me see."

"Your hands are so warm, young man."

"Yes, I've been told that, before."

"The pain has been getting much worse in the last few months since they won't cover my medicine anymore."

"So you stopped taking your medicine? Did the insurance company tell you why they won't pay?"

"No, they didn't say. I just got a letter. And the drug store charges too much now. I can't afford it."

"Here, let me try something, Mrs. Romero."

Jesus put his hands in the dirt and rubbed them together. Then he took the old woman's hands in his. "Now, please don't say anything. We must be quiet."

After a few minutes, Jesus let go and said, "Okay, that should do it. How do your hands feel?"

"Very good. Was it the heat from your hands? Should I start using a heating pad now?"

"I don't think that'll be necessary, Mrs. Romero," said Jesus with a smile. "I feel pretty good about this. You probably won't have any more problems with arthritis."

"What? Really?"

"Uh-huh. If that's the case, you'll know in a few days. And please don't tell anyone. I don't want others thinking I'm a faith healer, because it doesn't always work."

"Thank you, my boy. God bless you."

"You're welcome."

Jesus then got on his bike, held up his hand with the Vulcan salute, smiled and said, "I'll see you later." Then he rode off.

At the next meeting of the sewing circle, there was a notable absence.

"Where's Patty?" asked Sybil.

"She's not coming back," said Lily. "Good riddance if you ask me."

"Yes, good riddance," said Bertha.

"By the way, I met with Jesus Garcia," Lily announced.

"You did? Why did you do that?"

"I wanted to hear it for myself. And I'm telling you that he is a very bad man. He believes in evolution! He believes in climate change! And he's Catholic!"

As Lily continued talking, she got red in the face, her pupils dilated, and her normally blue eyes turned darker. "He wants to change everything. He thinks oil and gas are bad. He wants us to move to wind and solar. And now that he's been promoted into management, he'll be able to take the company in that direction."

"Oh, but he's only in the first rung," said Aline. "He won't be able to do anything there."

"Well, we're not going to take any chances. We need to neutralize him. Then we'll get rid of him."

"Okay, what should we do?" asked Sybil.

"Let's start saying he's threatening our jobs and that our salaries will be reduced if we move toward renewables."

"Where do we start?"

"In Administration. Those are the people we know best."

"We're going to need more information if people are going to believe us and spread the word. What else did he say in your meeting that we can use?"

"Actually, he led me to believe he has some stock in renewable energies."

"What! Oh, my God!" said Bertha. "Can you imagine? He's just trying to make himself rich."

"Yes, and by using our company to do it! What else did he say?"

"Oh, he said all kinds of other disturbing things. I'll make a list and get them to you."

"Good!"

"We also need to do some research, look into his background, and get some dirt on him. Maybe we can find what companies he's invested in."

"I'll give it to Mason," said Sybil. "He's good with computers and research. If it's out there, he'll find it."

Mesmerized by Lily, and believing everything she said was true, the sewing circle began spreading all kinds of rumors and lies about Jesus – and the gossip mill of human nature took over from there. Employees started whispering when they saw Jesus, telling false stories about him, and mocking him behind his back. Pretty soon, Lily's misleading narrative took on a life of its own and grew into all kinds of outrageous nonsense. Soon, the lies were believed by most. But only one person – Lily – knew the truth. And she seemed to revel in her own wickedness.

Jesus continued to hold small meetings with Global employees who had open minds. But he would meet one-on-one with skeptics, in part, because he thought personal conversation would be far more persuasive. One thing he discussed with everybody was that climate change was already happening. Because of rising sea levels, streets in low-lying coastal areas were flooding during king tides – and he showed them pictures of it happening in South Florida. "Scientists are predicting that, with time, this will be a daily occurrence," said

Jesus. "And not just in Florida, but in all low-lying coastal areas everywhere around the world."

Jesus advocated that rather than business as usual, everyone should look for new ways to ensure that homes, infrastructure, and drinking water aquifers survive the coming onslaught. "Remember the parable of the wise and foolish builders?" he would say. *"For the man who built his house on a foundation of rock, when a flood came, the torrent could not destroy his house.* But because of climate change, that is no longer true. In fact, that man would today be considered a foolish builder. The wise builder, rather, would be aware of how fast the seas are rising and construct his house farther inland and perhaps on stilts."

Jesus also suggested that "we need to find new and creative ways to deal with climate change. Remember what Einstein said: 'The significant problems we have cannot be solved at the same level of thinking with which we created them.'"

Pretty soon, a number of scientists and engineers who had previously been afraid to speak out for fear of losing their jobs, came to Jesus and presented new ideas that might be used to combat climate change. They included: a new kind of car battery that would get 1,000 miles on a single charge; additional ways to sequester and utilize carbon before it gets into the atmosphere; painting all rooftops white to reflect sunlight; building giant mirrors and placing them in space orbit; and a new type of solar battery that could be used to charge nearly all electronic devices, including mobile phones.

When Global Energy's executives heard that such ideas were being discussed internally, they were not pleased. Most now had a jaded view of their star oil and gas finder. He was simply becoming too controversial for them to stomach. And it didn't help matters when Jesus began warning people to "be on their guard against all kinds of greed." It was greed, he said, that drove corporations to construct high rise buildings in low-lying coastal areas – or to ramp up hydraulic fracking around the world, which would dramatically add to CO_2 emissions in the atmosphere. And he continued to talk to employees about being good shepherds of the earth, which frustrated people like Lily and the sewing circle. "God's first instruction to humanity was to 'serve and protect' the earth, to 'till and keep it,'" Jesus said. "Can we honestly say we are doing that?"

At the regular early morning get together, Madeleine and Pete warned Jesus about the bad vibes going around the office. "It's all coming from the sewing circle," said Pete.

"Actually, they knit," Jesus said with a wink.

"They do?"

"Yes," said Madeleine. "They knit."

"Okay, the 'knitting circle" is stirring people up by deliberately lying about your message."

"I know," said Jesus.

"You do? How do you know?"

"I know."

"Okay, well, they're saying all kinds of crazy things. "You believe in evolution. You're blasphemous. You're a Catholic. You're gay. You own stock in renewable energy companies. You're rude. You swear too much. You take the Lord's name in vain."

"Now, that's a good one," said Jesus laughing out loud.

"This is awful," said Madeleine. "How could they say such things?"

"Oh, it's okay," replied Jesus. "Human nature. I've seen it before. We have to expect it"

"Well, I don't think it's okay," replied Madeleine. "It's like they're out to get you. For crying out loud, we don't have to put up with that."

"How does something like this even start?" asked Pete.

"Oh, it's usually one person, a charismatic-type leader," said Jesus. "And that person typically stays in the background and has other people do the dirty work. That way they can deny direct responsibility and blame it on others if something goes wrong."

"Lily! That's Lily!" said Patty, who had joined the group. "That's how she operates!"

"Oh, yes!" Madeleine agreed. "Did you ever see her eyes? When she gets going, they look wild."

"She lies, too. And when her lies are discovered, she lies even more."

"And she never admits she's wrong. Never."

"She's single, isn't she?"

"Yes, I don't think she's ever been married, either."

"Okay," interrupted Jesus. "Let's not go there. All the negative things they're saying begin with simple gossip, you know."

"Oh?"

"Yes. Gossip is born out of selfishness. When people don't have anything else to do, or they're just lazy, they frequently spend their time gossiping or getting into other people's business. It wakes them up and puts them in a position of judging others. It can be especially bad in a group where people feed off each other, get excited, and then the talk often becomes hateful. And hate, of course, can lead to some evil deeds – like taking decent people down."

"But why do they do it?"

"Because it makes them feel good. It makes them feel superior to those they target – the people who won't gossip, who won't play their game, who won't join their group. And they have to be in a group, because they don't dare take action alone. They're afraid to. Just like they're afraid to disagree with the leader, or any other member of the group, for that matter.

"If left unchecked, smaller evil deeds can escalate to larger ones, including violence. And it's the group that causes it to happen. Taking others down, even to the point of killing them. And being in the group also disguises their extreme selfishness, which can cross the line to true evil."

"'If left unchecked' is the key phrase there," said Pete.

"Oh, yes," concluded Jesus. "It has to be dealt with, because true evil never rests. And it's everywhere – lurking behind the walls, in the shadows, in the fog, even in some of the offices in our own building. It can be on us in an instant – and then it's gone as fast as it appeared. And few people ever know the truth behind what happened."

Later that day, Sybil walked into Lily's office with Mason, who was carrying a manila folder. "We found something," said Sybil. "And it's big."

"Here, look at this," said Mason, as he opened the file and explained its contents to Lily.

Sybil closed the office door as the three spent the next ten minutes pouring over the papers and discussing what Mason had uncovered in his computer research.

"Oh, this is great! This is great!" said Lily. "Have you shown it to anybody else?"

"No," replied Mason. "We're the only ones who know."

"Good, let's keep it that way for now. I know exactly what to do and how to handle this."

Lily picked up the phone and dialed. While waiting for the connection, she waved Sybil and Mason out of her office. "Hello, it's Lily. Is he available? I need to come up and see him right away."

"Well, he's in a meeting right now," came the reply. "But I can squeeze you in for a few minutes at three o'clock."

"Thank you. I'll see you at three."

At 3:00 PM on the dot, Lily walked into the executive vice president's suite and was immediately waved through.

"Knock, knock," she said as she got to his office door.

"Hello, Lily, come on in. Is this about the company picnic, again? I thought we had settled what kind of mustard we were going to use on the hot dogs."

"Yes, we did, sir. This is about something else."

"Okay, come in and sit down. What is it?"

"Well, I agonized about whether to bring this to you," said Lily, "because, as you know, I don't like to say negative things about people."

"Um, hm. Um, hm."

"But I thought this was just too important."

"Yes?"

"Well, I did some research online and . . . ."

"Get to the point, will you, please."

"Yes, sir. It appears that Jesus Garcia is an illegal immigrant."

"What?"

"Yes, sir. He and his family unlawfully moved from Mexico to California," said Lily, as she opened the file and put it on the desk. "He has no birth certificate that I can find. I don't know how he got a social security number."

There were a few moments of silence as the executive flipped through the papers. "Are you sure about this?"

"Absolutely," replied Lily. "The documents don't lie – or the lack of documents, if you will."

After another pause from the executive, he asked, "What else do you know about him?"

"Well, he lives on the east side of town in a shack. He works in a church with homeless people. Somebody I know saw him down on skid row talking to prostitutes."

"Why does he associate with those low-life people?"

"I don't know," replied Lily. "But with all his talk about global warming, a lot of our employees think he is disparaging the industry. The rumor floating around is that he has a lot of stock in a company that makes solar panels."

"Hmmm . . . . Well, okay. Thank you for bringing this to me Lily. I'll get back to you."

Shortly after Jesus arrived at work the next morning, Nick walked into his office and closed the door. "We have a problem, kid," he said.

Nick then explained that word had reached the senior executives about Jesus being an undocumented immigrant. "They're saying that you illegally crossed the border with your family. And they're speculating that you have a fake social security number. They're gunning for you, kid. You're going to be called up to the board room in a few minutes."

"I see," replied Jesus. "Thanks for the heads up."

As Nick left, Jesus placed a call to his mother in Los Angeles. She explained that when Jesus was five, they had all moved to Los

Angeles from Mexico City. His uncle, who had crossed the border a few years earlier, found people who could create fake birth certificates, which were later used to obtain social security numbers.

"We wanted to have you start school in the United States by the first grade," she said. "I'm sorry we never told you. We should have. But we thought you would be too young to remember, and it wouldn't matter, anyway."

"Are you and father undocumented also?" asked Jesus.

"Yes."

"No Green Cards?

"No."

"Okay, Mother. Don't tell me anything more. I have to go."

Seven top-level executives were assembled in the boardroom when Jesus walked in. They were all seated on one side of the table. He sat alone on the other side. The Human Resources vice president started the conversation. "Jesus, we've been told that you weren't born in the United States and are undocumented. Is that true?"

"Yes, it is," replied Jesus.

There was a brief silence.

"I see. May I ask how old you were when you came to this country?"

"Five, I believe."

"So you were too young to remember?" said Nick.

Jesus smiled but did not respond.

"Well, how in the world did you get a social security number if you were born in Mexico?" asked one of the vice presidents.

"I really don't have the details on that," Jesus replied.

There was another pause, this one longer.

Then the senior VP to whom Lily reported leaned forward. "You know, son, a lot of people are upset that you talk so forthrightly about global warming being a danger."

"Yes, I know. But I have spoken openly and done nothing in secret."

"Some think your rhetoric might harm the company."

"Well, sir," replied Jesus, "I would suggest that the changing climate is also a threat to the industry, as a whole. In the recent storm, for instance, a quarter of our onshore oil and gas production was shut down and our offshore operations in the Gulf were severely damaged."

"Many employees are concerned that too much talk of global warming is a threat their to their jobs."

"Yes, sir, I am aware of that, also. But our company can be a global leader on this issue. We can say to the world that climate change is, indeed, a major problem. And we can start doing something about it right now by committing to a gradual switch to renewable energies. And that will create more than enough jobs for everybody."

There was another long pause as the executives looked around at each other.

"Well, Mr. Garcia, this issue of you being undocumented is very serious," said Curtis, the president of the company. Do you have anything else to say for yourself."

"No sir, I do not."

"Okay, then. We'll get back to your shortly."

Jesus quickly exited the room.

"All right, men, what do we do with this guy?" asked the president.

"Well, we all heard him admit that he's illegal, didn't we? He has to go."

"I agree."

"But we just promoted him," said the HR vice president. "And he's our best grease finder. Do we really want to let that go?"

Then Nick jumped in: "I don't think this young man is at fault here," he said. "His parents, maybe, but not him."

"Oh, he had to know. These people have strong family circles. They tell each other everything."

"Yeah, he's lying."

"No, I don't think he is," said Nick. "He admitted it, for Christ's sake! And let me put something else out there. His recommendation for us to take the lead on climate change and make a gradual switch to renewables is a pretty good idea. If we got after it, we could make it happen in a decade or so."

"Yeah, but that would take a big initial investment, which would cut into our yearly profits," said one of the executive vice presidents. "And besides, we'll probably all be retired in ten years."

The meeting lasted for another thirty minutes or so, right after which, Nick walked into Jesus's office, closed the door, and slumped down into a chair.

"Well?" asked Jesus.

"Well, they're giving you a chance to resign. A month's severance. And it has to be right now. If you don't take it, you'll be out with nothing but your matching contributions."

Jesus swiveled his chair and looked out the window up toward the clouds for a few moments.

"Okay," he said, turning back toward Nick. "I'm gone. Will you let them know for me."

"Sure, kid, I'll take care of it," he replied as he stood up to leave.

"Oh, Nick," said Jesus. "Thanks for supporting me in there."

Nick just nodded, looked down, and walked back to his office.

Jesus didn't waste any time. He packed a cardboard box with some of his things and headed for the elevator. On the way down, the doors opened, and a short middle-aged woman stepped on. She looked up, frowned and said: "Are you Jesus?"

"Yes, ma'am."

The woman then slapped him hard on the left side of the face. "Take that," she said.

His eyes watering, Jesus did not respond, but simply turned his head, which made the woman so mad that she back-slapped him on his right cheek.

"Damn you!" she shouted.

Then the elevator doors opened at a lower level and she walked off.

During the lunch break that day, Lily walked into the sewing circle with her eyes beaming bright blue. "It's time to celebrate," she shrieked. "They fired him!"

"Really?" asked Sybil.

"Yes, indeed. I saw him leaving the office carrying his stuff."

Most of the women shouted and high-fived each other.

"Good riddance to that Mexican!" one of them said.

"He had it coming," said another.

Aline stood up and headed for the door. "There is nothing to celebrate here!" she said, before walking out. "And by the way, my husband is Latino."

That evening at the Church of Our Lady of Guadalupe, Jesus was in the first pew looking up at the image of the Virgin Mary, when Father Miguel walked over and sat down next to him. "Are you all right, my son?" he asked. Not taking his eyes off the altar, and without changing expression, Jesus nodded his head up and down slightly.

"Good. There are some people here to see you."

Jesus then turned toward Father Miguel, who tapped him on the leg and said, "Come along."

Waiting for them in the priest's office were Pete, Madeleine, and Rodrigo. One at a time, they embraced Jesus. "Word got around the office pretty quick this afternoon," said Pete. "And a lot of people are very upset."

"The three of us have quit Global," Madeleine announced. "We don't want to work for a company that would treat a good person like you in such a way. Any one of us could be next."

"What! Really? Rodrigo?" asked Jesus knowing full well how much a good paying job meant to him.

"Si, you también," he replied. "There are other jobs."

Now speechless, tears rolled down Jesus's cheeks.

Father Miguel broke the silence. "Come, everybody, let's go to dinner. It's on me."

"Good idea," said Madeleine.

"Si, tengo hambre," said Rodrigo.

"I never pass up a free meal!" quipped Pete, as everybody smiled. "C'mon Jesus."

When the five sat down at a nearby casual dining restaurant, the priest immediately ordered a Scotch on the rocks.

"Miguel!" said Jesus.

"Don't look so surprised," came the reply. "Catholic priests are not allowed to get married. We're not allowed to swear. Heck, there are a lot of things we're not allowed to do. But we ARE allowed to drink. And it's time for a drink!"

"Now this is my kind of priest!" said Pete. "I'll have a beer."

"Me, too," said Madeleine. "Whatever's on tap."

"Cerveza!" shouted Rodrigo slapping the table.

"Come on, Jesus."

"Oh, my mother and father won't like this. But okay. One beer."

Father Miguel looked up toward the ceiling and quipped, "Forgive him, Father, for he knows not what he does." And everybody laughed.

Talk at the table during dinner and drinks began with the scurrilous actions of the corporate executives. "They're all men, all white, all greedy," said Madeleine. "They'd fire anyone if they thought their bonuses might be negatively affected. It just makes me so mad."

"I'm not angry, just a little depressed," lamented Jesus. "I bear no ill will toward them. As the scripture says, *'My yoke is easy and my burden is light.'*"

"You're amazing," said Madeleine. "They just fired you and you're so calm."

"Actually, it's good that I'm gone from there. I shouldn't be in this business, anyway. I'm good at finding oil and gas, but that only contributes to the problem. I need to make amends."

The group then began talking about pooling their efforts to form a new organization to raise awareness about the changing climate and the dangers associated with it. The time was right, they all agreed. They'd start by using money from their own savings to get going, then they would seek donations and continue to build. Father Miguel offered to let his church be the headquarters. And all agreed that Jesus should be the main presenter, not only because he was a good speaker, but he also explained science in a way that everybody could understand.

"Do you think people will buy in?" asked Madeleine.

"I do," replied Pete. Actually I think we're going to have a good amount of support – even from inside our own company."

"Former company!" Madeleine reminded him.

"Yes, our former company!" said Pete, hoisting his glass. "Cheers!"

"I'll drink to that," said Father Miguel, who was feeling no pain from the evening's scotch after scotch.

Jesus, too, had forgotten himself and had one too many beers. In fact, he got seriously inebriated for the first time in his life. Eventually, he started singing the song *Everything's Alright.*

After he sang the first few verses about not being worried or upset and that everything was going to be okay, Pete leaned into Father Miguel and whispered: "Where's that coming from?"

"From Jesus Christ, Superstar, I think."

And Jesus continued singing, now a bit louder, about calming and anointing people, about soon "feeling" better, and about "everything" eventually being "alright."

Finally, Father Miguel rose from the table. "I have a "feeling" it's time to go," he said. So Pete and Rodrigo got on either side of Jesus, pulled him up, and then started out of the restaurant. A smiling Jesus raised his hand toward the people at one table as if to anoint them, and said: "Blessed are they who hunger and thirst for righteousness, for they shall be satisfied.

"Blessed are the meek, for they shall inherit the earth," he said to another.

As the patrons began cheering and laughing, Pete and Rodrigo sped up their movement toward the front door. And Jesus started speaking faster. "Blessed are the poor in spirit . . . . Blessed are the pure of heart . . . . Blessed are the peacemakers. . . . Blessed are the . . . ." When they got through the door to the street, Jesus said: "Wait a minute, wait a minute, I'm not done."

"Yes you are," said Pete. "You're done."

"But there are a few more."

"Okay, okay, so you know the Beatitudes," said Madeleine. "We're impressed."

"I'll take him home with me," said Rodrigo, wrapping Jesus's arm around his neck. "Esta a la vuelta de la esquina; it's right around the corner. Besides, if it weren't for him, I wouldn't even have a place to go tonight."

As they walked down the street, Jesus started singing again – and Rodrigo joined in.

True to his word, Father Miguel designated a small office on the grounds of Our Lady of Guadalupe for the group. It had three desks, a computer, printer, coffee maker, and several extra chairs. Jesus spent nearly all of his time there preparing a new major presentation. He was determined to lay out the basics of climate change science, place the responsibility squarely where it belonged, foretell what the future would hold if things continued on the present course, and inspire people to take action.

Meanwhile, Pete, Madeleine, Rodrigo, and Patty (who was working part time with the group) made plans to hold the first major presentation in a downtown Houston park. They secured permission to use a concert stage, which was built on a slight promontory near a sizeable man-made lake. They would hold the event at noon on a normal business working day. And Jesus would speak and answer questions from the audience.

That spring day, hundreds of people were sitting on the grass and milling about the park. Many had brought sack lunches or purchased something to eat from one of the many vendors in the park. Surprised by the size of the crowd, Jesus took the stage by himself, turned on the microphone, and began speaking.

"Climate change is real," he began. "*We The People* are causing climate change."

Jesus paused a moment, as much of the crowd moved toward him. "Today, I'm going to tell you the story of an unbroken chain that begins with us. *We The People* are causing climate change mainly by using fossil fuels for electricity, heat, and transportation.

"Our use of fossil fuels causes an increase of carbon dioxide (CO_2) in the atmosphere.

"This is a scientific truth. "Since the beginning of the modern industrial revolution in the mid-to late-nineteenth century, CO_2 amounts in the air have risen consistently and are now rising unbelievably fast. A graph of the most recent historical data looks something like a hockey stick, with the tip going almost straight up.

"Carbon Dioxide is a gas that absorbs heat. The more CO_2 in the atmosphere, the more the sun's heat is absorbed. More heat in the atmosphere drives temperatures up.

"So the increase of CO_2 in the earth's atmosphere causes rising temperatures around the world. This also is a scientific truth. Since the start of the industrial age, the average global surface temperature has risen about 2 degrees Fahrenheit.

"Rising temperatures cause more evaporation.

"This is a scientific fact. "Evaporation is a process where liquid water changes to water vapor due to an increase in temperature.

"More evaporation causes there to be more moisture in the atmosphere. Remember that moisture is simply water vapor.

"So <u>more moisture in the atmosphere causes more rain and more flooding</u>.

"<u>Rising temperatures on the land cause a disruption of weather patterns, droughts, forest fires, flash flooding, stronger tornadoes, and inland hurricanes</u>.

"<u>Hotter temperatures on the oceans, cause more and stronger hurricanes and longer hurricane seasons</u>.

"<u>Hotter temperatures cause ice to melt</u>.

"And <u>melting ice causes sea level to rise</u>.

"This is a scientific truth. Just as icicles melt when they get warm, ice at the North Pole (the Arctic), ice at the South Pole (Antarctica), and the Greenland ice sheet are melting, because it's getting hotter outside. And glaciers, which are made mostly of ice, are also melting all around the world.

"<u>Hotter temperatures</u> also <u>cause water to expand</u>.

"This is a scientific fact. It's called thermal expansion where warm water expands and occupies more space than cooler water. The more space water occupies, the higher sea levels rise.

"So, <u>melting ice and water expansion cause sea level to rise</u>.

"And <u>sea level rise causes coastal flooding</u>.

"This is a scientific fact. "Just like when you drop ice cubes into a cup of soda, the soda rises, then they melt and add water to the drink. So it is that melting icebergs are breaking off ice sheets and dropping into our oceans. If all of the Greenland ice sheet melted, sea level would go up 20 feet, which would submerge a third of the City of New York. If Antarctica melted, along with all of the ice on earth, global seal level rise would be 262 feet. And that would place water above the waist on the Statue of Liberty. Many of the world's most populous cities would be inundated. Every city on the eastern coast of the United States and every city on the Gulf of Mexico would be submerged. The entire state of Florida would disappear. And Houston, where we are standing right now, would be 100 feet below the surface of the sea.

"So unless people can find a way to live underwater, we're all eventually going to have to move. Right? If sea levels rise to these levels, we will experience a gradual loss of fresh drinking water aquifers due to saltwater contamination. And of course we will experience a gradual loss of land to live on. So people will have to move. Right?"

"Right!" answered people in the crowd.

"And as the earth gets hotter, because of droughts, we'll gradually lose the ability to farm and grow food. We may also reach a temperature so hot we simply will not be able to survive. In that case, people will have to move. Right?"

"Right!"

"So we may see a gradual displacement of very large populations – millions, perhaps billions of people worldwide. And the immigration crises we're experiencing today will worsen to a scale that has never been seen in human history.

"So let's recap the eight unbroken links in this powerful chain.

1. *The use of fossil fuels increases CO2 in the atmosphere.*

2. *More CO2 in the atmosphere causes temperatures to rise.*

3. *Rising temperatures cause more evaporation, which leads to more moisture in the atmosphere, which causes more rain and more flooding.*

4. *Rising temperatures on the land cause a disruption of weather patterns, droughts, forest fires, flooding, stronger tornadoes, and inland hurricanes.*

5. *Rising temperatures on the oceans cause more and stronger hurricanes and longer hurricane seasons.*

6. *Rising temperatures cause ice to melt and water to expand.*

7. *Melting ice and water expansion cause sea level to rise.*

8. *Sea level rise causes coastal flooding, loss of land, and mass migrations.*

"I wonder if this reminds you, as it does me, of the old proverb:

For want of a nail the shoe was lost.
For want of a shoe the horse was lost.
For want of a horse the rider was lost.

For want of a rider the battle was lost.
For want of a battle the kingdom was lost.
And all for the want of a horseshoe nail.

"Well, if not for people using fossil fuels, ... you get my point.

"Now recall, if you will, what it says in the New Testament: *In the days before the flood, people were eating, drinking, and marrying . . . and they knew nothing about what would happen until the flood came and took them all away.*"

"Well, thanks to science, today we know what is going to happen. So let's not wait until the floods come and sweep us all away. Let us remain watchful, be alert, and prepare.

"And let's begin to break the chain and stop the cause of climate change. We can all be a part of healing the earth by fixing the problem we, ourselves, created. One thing we can do is to look for new ideas – ideas that can be used to ensure that our homes and families will be safe. We can, for example, transition from fossil fuels to renewable energies.

"To do this, however, we must stand up to the oil and gas companies that are still exploring for and producing fossil fuels at an unprecedented rate. Why do they continue to do so? They have scientists on staff who know the truth. They understand the damage they're doing. The answer is money – the root of all evil.

"Ladies and gentlemen, *We the People* started the chain of events that causes climate change. And *We the People* can end it. Remember, the earth has a remarkable ability to heal itself. All we have to do is help it along. Please join me . . . please join *us* in trying to make things right.

"Thank you very much.

"Now, we have some time for a few questions or comments."

Pete, Madeleine, and Aline were out in the crowd with microphones. The first person to speak didn't look too pleased. "I don't believe it!" he said. "I don't believe *you*. And by the way, I work for an oil and gas company and I am not the enemy!"

"Of course you're not the enemy," replied Jesus. "But everyone has a right to know the truth. And please don't take my word for it. I encourage everybody to study the issue for yourselves. I think you'll find that the science is solid. And by the way, I believe our scientists can help make the world a better place. We must listen to them, follow their advice, and teach their truths to the world."

"How can we contact you and get involved?" asked another person.

"Well, we just got started and we're based at Our Lady of Guadalupe Catholic Church. You can reach us there."

After a few more comments, Jesus thanked the crowd for listening, gave the Vulcan salute, and walked off the stage.

The next morning about fifty people showed up at the church offering to volunteer their time. The presentation resonated with much of the crowd because of what they had gone through with the previous year's storm. Many individuals, in fact, were still staying in shelters waiting for their homes to be repaired or rebuilt. Later that day, a number of articles were written about Jesus's speech – and the church was soon flooded with phone calls and social media requests asking how to donate.

Pete, Madeleine, and Rodrigo were overwhelmed with all the activity. They decided it was time to expand. So Father Miguel gave them another room in the church and some extra furniture to accommodate all the volunteers, many of whom brought their own phones and computers. It wasn't enough, however.

"We need a new, more aggressive plan," advocated Madeleine. "We should take our message on the road – only this time we use a computer presentation with photographs and charts based on the latest research."

"Yes," agreed Pete. "Jesus will put one together for us to use as a template."

"By the way, where has he wandered off to this time?" asked Pete.

"California," said Rodrigo. "He wanted to see that forest fire near Los Angeles for himself – para checar y ver a su familia; to check in on his family."

"Oh, I was reading about that this morning," said Pete. "Fifty thousand homes evacuated, a quarter of a million people, over 400 structures destroyed. Mansions in Malibu got hit pretty hard."

"Oh, my goodness. Now I'm worried. Knowing Jesus, he'll get too close."

"Estoy seguro de que estará bien; I'm sure he'll be fine. He said he'd contact us in a day or two."

Immediately upon his return, Jesus received a call from Nick asking to meet privately.

"Well, tomorrow, Father Miguel and I are having breakfast at a small café near the cancer hospital," he replied. "If you don't mind him being there, why don't you join us."

"Okay. I guess a priest can keep a secret."

The next morning, when the three met, Nick pulled some papers out of his briefcase and put them on the table. "Okay," he said to Jesus, "I called in a favor and arranged to set you up for temporary legal status. Here are documents for you to fill out and sign. I'll need them by tomorrow morning. These will protect you from deportation. I also have an application for a Green Card and, as of now, I think we can get it through without any hassle. I told my friend that you have three advanced degrees, no criminal record, and lots of people who will vouch for you. He said he might be able to get it on the fast track and, if so, it should sail through.

"Oh, and Father," Nick said, "If you could please keep this between us, I'd be grateful. I'm already in enough hot water at the company for believing in Jesus."

"Okay," replied the priest.

"Thank you for this, Nick," said Jesus.

"You bet, kid. This was no fault of your own, but I'm afraid your parents might be at risk. So we're going to need to get some things going to protect them."

"Yes, I talked to them about it when I was in L.A. They're worried."

"Oh, and by the way," Jesus went on, "I just received a letter from the government saying, "It has come to our attention . . . .   I guess somebody reported it."

"It was probably Lily," said Nick. "Or she had one of her stooges do it. She's still stirring up trouble at work. She's evil. Sorry, Father, but she's telling all kinds of lies about Jesus. It's awful."

"She that troubleth her own house shall inherit the wind," said Father Miguel.

Jesus smiled when he heard one of his favorite biblical quotes. "You know, that word 'evil' is touchy. It means different things to different people. The worst, of course, is killing somebody."

"Well, I hate to say this, but I think she's capable of that."

"You might be too strong, there, Nick," cautioned Jesus. "She's definitely capable of killing the truth and lying, but that's probably the extent of it."

"So you wouldn't call her evil?"

"Capable of lesser evil deeds, I'd say. But we all are."

"Oh?" asked Nick.

"We all have to balance the good and evil in ourselves," replied Jesus. "Actually, it would be better if we called it balancing the 'selfish' and 'unselfish.' The more unselfish we are, the more we're prone to do good – just as selfish individuals are more prone to do evil."

"It can be a lifelong journey to strive toward goodness," said Jesus. "Some people come close near the end of their lives. But most stop striving somewhere along the way, for various reasons."

"I'm trying to be a better person," said Nick.

"Well, I think you're on the right path," said Father Miguel. "A person's goodness is made obvious when interacting with others and being honest in all things."

"A good person produces good words from a good heart," said Jesus. "We speak of what we know and bear witness to what we have seen. You, sir, have a good heart."

"I agree," said Father Miguel.

"Well, thank you," Nick replied. "But I'm working for a company that is harming the earth."

"So was I," said Jesus. "I was trying to change it from within. Now you can take the lead on that."

"Easier said than done," said Nick. "Besides, I not only have to work on these dogmatic people, but on myself, too. It's a real struggle."

"Well, I know you can handle the executives at Global," said Jesus. "As for your own personal journey toward goodness, I'd advise going back and reading the Gospels. See if you gain some insights that you did not see when you were younger. I think you will.

"And remember what the poet said," concluded Jesus: "Of all the forms of genius, goodness has the longest awkward age."

Nick took a sip of coffee as he pondered the meaning of that quote.

"Oh, by the way," he said, "I attended your rally last month. It was terrific."

"Yeah, things have been really snowballing," Jesus replied.

"You can say that, again," said Nick. "We've expanded in the church thanks to Father Miguel. We now have hundreds of volunteers, money coming in from all over. We'll use your computer presentation as a base for people to go out and spread the word. And we think it'll inspire others to set up groups in some other cities and states."

"That's great – and my presentation is ready," said Jesus.

"Pete, Madeleine, and Rodrigo are taking the lead. And they're finding that young people, especially, are responding – college and high school students, adolescents, even young children."

"No kidding?" asked Father Miguel.

"Yes! Young children! I knew they'd come on board," said Jesus. "Once we tell them the truth in a way they can understand, they want to help. I tell you, if we all became like a little child, this would be a better world."

"Speaking of children," said Father Miguel. "We'd better get going."

"Oh, yes," said Jesus. "Come, Nick. Walk with us."

The three walked a few blocks over to the children's cancer hospital and went up to the third floor where they met the head nurse. "They're all waiting for you in the play room," she said. "Usually, it's a very quiet place here in the mornings, the kids are lethargic, and it can be very depressing. But they're all up now, have had breakfast, and love visitors. Oh, one more thing, these children have the worst diagnoses, very advanced stages for the most part. I just wanted to make sure you knew."

Jesus walked over to a table and opened his backpack while Father Miguel began setting up a computer and projector. Nick stood in the back and watched.

"Children, this is Mr. Jesus Garcia," said the nurse. "He's going to talk to you about science and climate change."

"Hi, everybody, it's nice to be with you," Jesus began. "We're going start by having some fun with magnets this morning. You all know what magnets are, don't you."

"Yes," said one little boy. "We have them on the fridge at home."

"Right. Well, here is a big horseshoe-shaped magnet and it will pick up these paper clips and many other things made of metal. Here's a rock with a lot of iron in it. See how it picks up the rock?"

"How does it do that?"

"Well, it's caused by special energy that we call a magnetic field. It's invisible, which means we have to believe in something we can't see."

"Like God?" asked a child.

Jesus only smiled and said, "I want to tell you a story. I first became interested in magnetic fields back when I was about your age. I met a priest who had a special energy in his hands and, sometimes, when he touched people, their aches and pains went away. And when he touched my arm I could feel some warmth and a kind of swirling motion. The priest said he thought it was some sort of magnetic field. I had never felt anything like that before and it made me curious, so I started studying magnets."

One of the kids raised his hand. "Could the priest touch people and cure cancer?" he asked.

"You know, maybe one day, a magnetic field might be able to help with a cure," replied Jesus.

"Now, let me demonstrate that magnetic fields really do exist," he continued. "Just watch this." Jesus pulled out of his bag a plastic plate that was about four inches square and one inch deep, plugged it in, and held a one inch round metal disk over it. Then he let go and the disk floated about three inches above the plate.

"Whoa!" said the kids who started to crowd around.

"You see, magnets can both attract and repel metal. In this case, the magnets in the plate are configured just right so that the field they produce repels the metal disk and makes it float in mid air," said Jesus. "Watch, I can run my hand between the plate and disk, and the magnetic field will not be broken. The disk will hold some weight, too." Jesus then alternately placed a pen, a watch, and a plastic cup with some orange juice in it on top of the disk.

"And look at this," he said, as he put a small toy frog on the disk. "If we place it just off center, it spins."

"Wow! Cool!" marveled the children.

"The electrical current we get by plugging it in, creates a magnetic field in the very strong magnets. And since there is energy in a magnetic field, we are able to capture it and use it for what we want – in this case, to make the frog float and spin.

"You see, this is just one of many parts of science. And science can be really fun."

"Jesus," said Father Miguel. "The presentation is ready to go."

"Thank you, Father. Now, kids, I want to show you another aspect of science. And this one relates to the earth and how the earth's environment is changing."

For the next fifteen minutes, Jesus talked to the children about the facts, causes, and impacts surrounding climate change. He used mostly photographs and spoke in very simple language that everyone could understand. And toward the end, he mentioned using solar and wind power instead of oil and gas to help make things better.

One little girl's hand shot up. "Can we use the energy in magnetic fields, too?" she asked.

"That's a good question," Jesus replied. "There have been experiments at major universities on that very subject. In fact, magnetic fields are already being used to make electric cars go."

"You mean like a Tesla?"

"Yes, indeed. Just like a Tesla."

"Cool!"

"Okay, kids, that concludes our presentation," said Jesus. "I hope that when you grow up, you will consider becoming scientists. If you do, then maybe you can come up with a new invention that will help solve climate change. Remember, just one great idea can save the world."

As the children filed out, Father Miguel and Nick packed up the computer, projector, and the magnets while Jesus stood over to the side speaking with the head nurse. After they finished, Nick and Miguel turned toward the elevators, but Jesus called out, "This way, guys."

"Where are we going?" asked Nick.

"We're going to visit the kids in their rooms."

So for the next couple of hours, right up until lunch, the three together wandered around to each of the children. Most appeared more pale and gaunt once they were back in bed. One little boy smiled broadly at first, but then got a serious look on his face. "Mr. Jesus, do you believe in God," he asked.

"Why do you ask?" replied Jesus.

"Well, my father doesn't believe in God anymore, because I got cancer and am going to die."

"I'm not so sure about you dying," said Jesus. "You can get well."

"My mother still believes," continued the boy. "She prays for God to cure me."

"Well, I'm sure her prayers are heard."

"I don't know. She cries all the time . . . all the time."

"Neither you or your mother or father must lose hope," said Jesus, leaning down and kissing the boy on the forehead. "You are the light of the world. Remember that."

Jesus went around and spoke to the rest of the children, asking each how they felt, where they were from, and what they wanted to be when they grew up. He touched them all, told them they mustn't lose hope, and said he would see them all again.

As the three men walked toward the elevators, Jesus once more stopped to talk to the head nurse.

"You know," Father Miguel whispered to Nick, "there's something very spiritual about our friend. Did you see how he connected with those children and how their faces lit up? He also can quote from the Bible better than anyone I've ever met. And he seems to know every word of the New Testament."

"Yes, I think he's got a photographic memory," Nick replied. "And his kindness is virtually unending."

"Okay," said Jesus. "I've spoken with the nurse and we're all set to visit the other two children's wards next week and the week after – same day, same time."

As the doors closed on the elevator, Jesus smiled and waved the Vulcan salute to the nurse.

Over the next sixth months so, Jesus's message on climate change began to take hold. More donations poured in, and volunteers popped up from all over the country, from every walk of life. Small groups formed spontaneously, held rallies, performed research, and crafted their own climate change speeches. Soon, local media covered the events and then Jesus and his organization began garnering national attention. Young people, especially, spoke out fearlessly against the oil and gas industry. Pressure was brought to bear on political leaders to accelerate the switch to renewable energies. More ideas for moving away from fossil fuels flowed into Mother of Guadalupe. They ranged from the simple to the extraordinary – everything from stopping unconventional oil and gas drilling and injecting toxic fracking fluids into the ground – to building more nuclear power plants. And there were numerous strategies presented for removing carbon dioxide from the atmosphere, just as plants and trees do. Some of those suggestions, included: better forest preservation and management; new farming practices that put more nutrients into the soil; and ocean farming of seaweed, which also pulls carbon from seawater.

All the while, the major oil and gas companies remained silent, continued to produce their products, and refused to acknowledge that there was even a problem. Angered by their inaction, Jesus intensified his attacks on the energy industry by going to several major media outlets. "They do nothing, they say nothing, they deny any responsibility," he charged. "And they pay outrageous sums of money to unethical scientists who claim that their own research proves that climate change is not real, that it is unfounded, and that it is nothing more than a hoax.

"The executives in these corporations are money-grubbers and liars!" Jesus said.

"No one can legitimately deny something so obvious as this changing climate and the science that proves it is being caused by the human race. *Ye can discern the face of the sky and of the earth, but how is it that you do not discern this time?* We were put here to care for the earth. It is our responsibility to protect and preserve it for future generations."

Then Jesus began calling for nothing less than a revolution. "Now is the time to challenge everything," he said. "We must change our thinking. Join us – and become part of a new movement!"

After dinner at the residence of Global Energy's president, the company's top five executives moved into the study and met behind closed doors. "Okay, we're here to deal with this Jesus kid," said Curtis. "I've been receiving calls all week from my friends in the industry and they are very upset."

"Well, no wonder," said one of the executive vice presidents. "He's still preaching a complete turn away from oil and gas toward renewables. Only now, it's on a national scale and people are beginning to buy in. Have you seen the crowds he's been drawing. They just keep getting bigger."

"Yeah, and he's targeting us now," said another. "Have you heard what he's been saying? We're responsible for all these storms and fires. We're destroying the planet. We're liars. We're evil."

"Did he really say that we're evil."

"Well, in one of his recent rants, he compared us to the wicked tenants in that New Testament story."

"What?"

"Yeah, he said we weren't taking care of the earth and we needed to be cast out of the vineyard."

"He keeps quoting the Bible against us. Like we're the anti-Christ, or something."

"And what is it with that Vulcan salute he always uses? Who does he think he is, Dr. Spock."

"*Mr.* Spock."

"What?"

"You know, from Star Trek."

"Whatever."

Curtis then took over the conversation. The company's president had an unusually loud, harsh, and irritating voice that punctuated his dominating personality. "I don't like him," he said. "This guy's an agitator. The growing crowds he's attracting really worry me. That can lead to influencing too many people in Washington, which could really harm us."

"So what do you want to do?"

"Well, clearly, there's only one thing to do, and that is to remove him permanently. If he's taken out, his movement will collapse."

The other executives in the room remained silent for a few moments. They could feel from the sound of their leader's voice that he was seriously locked in on killing Jesus. And none dared challenge him.

Finally, one of the executives spoke up. "Well, if we're going to do that, we'll have to set it up as an ambush. And we'll need a scapegoat, somebody we can blame."

"I was thinking that we need to get one of the low-lifes to do it for us," said Curtis.

"How about Lily?"

"Oh, Lily! Even I'm afraid of her. Have you seen that bitch's eyes?"

"Yeah, but she'd be great for this. She's riled up nearly the entire office. Almost everybody hates Jesus because of her. Did you know that her group actually wrote to USC, Stanford, and Harvard trying to get his degrees taken away – and tried to have the Immigration and Naturalization Service deport him."

"Lily did that?"

"Well, her people did. She doesn't do anything herself. She gets others to do it so she can't be blamed."

"Can she really get her people to take this on?"

"I think so. She's got some sort of Svengali-like hold over them. It's amazing."

"She'd be perfect, then. Do you think she'll work with us?"

"Oh, yeah. She hates Jesus."

"What would it take?"

"Power. Tell her we'll promote her to vice president. She's also greedy. Offer her money – and lots of it, so she can pay her cult."

"Well, we can certainly get as much cash as we need."

"Somebody will have to approach her to get it going."

"I'll do it myself," said Curtis.

"Good. She'll be flattered that the top guy came to her. She's got nothing else in her life and she's about as selfish a person as you can imagine."

A couple of day's later, Lily walked into the president's office. "Hello, sir. You asked to see me?"

"Yes, Lily," he said, getting up from his desk and shaking her hand. "It's nice to see you. Please take a seat over on the couch."

Curtis then closed the door and sat down in a chair next to her. After a few minutes of niceties and small talk, he laid out the entire situation and what they were looking to do.

"Lily, over the years, you've demonstrated your loyalty to Global in many ways," he said. "We value you as a member of our team. We're coming to you, because we believe you feel the same way about this Jesus fellow and the harm he is doing to our industry."

"Yes, I do," she replied. "But, sir, I have to ask what's in it for me?"

"Of course. If we can pull this off, you'll be promoted to vice president of administration, which means you'll run the whole show both nationally and internationally. And of course, that position comes with the commensurate salary and bonus structure."

"Hmmm," she replied.

Sensing the offer wasn't enough, Curtis then stated that there was lots of money involved.

"How much?"

"A million for you. A hundred thousand for anybody else you get to participate."

"Oh, wow!" she said, trying not to get too excited.

"Do you think that will be enough?" asked Curtis.

"Oh, yes. More than enough."

"Of course, it'll all be in cash. Clean money. Half now, half on completion."

Clearing her throat, Lily asked if a specific plan had been worked out.

"Right now, we are thinking of luring him back to the office for a presentation. Kind of a show of good will. He'll be taken out here."

"How are we going to get him to come back?"

"We'll get one of his friends here to invite him."

"He doesn't have very many friends here, sir."

"We have somebody in mind. We've also brought in a professional. He will be your contact and you will work directly through him. No one else."

"I see."

"Of course, all communication will be on a need-to-know basis."

"Of course."

"And none of this can ever get back to you, me, or the top echelon at Global."

"I understand."

"Is all this acceptable to you, Lily?"

"Oh, yes."

"So you're in."

"Yes, sir. I am all in."

"Good. You'll be contacted soon with more information and the first payment."

When Jesus walked into a local school for the deaf, he was greeted by the director and a red-headed eleven-year-old girl.

"Hello, young lady," he said, in sign language. "What beautiful hair you have."

"Thank you," she responded.

"What is your name?"

"I'm Cindy. Nice to have you with us today."

The two led their visitor to the building's atrium where about twenty or so students were gathered. After plugging his computer into the projection system and being introduced, Jesus gave his climate presentation to the children. The director, who was planning on interpreting, was surprised that Jesus knew sign language, so she just took a seat with the rest of the students. After fifteen minutes, he started talking about the wonders of science.

"Let me give you an example of how cool science can be," he began.

"Of course, we all know you can feel sound, right? We feel it through the vibrations. But did you know that you can also see sound?"

Then he pulled several items from his backpack and them set on the table – a stereo speaker, a black metal plate which he attached to the top of the speaker, and a miniature keyboard – all of which he plugged into his laptop. After sprinkling some white sand on top of the plate, Jesus asked the students to gather around so they could see better.

"Now, if we play different musical tones through the speaker, the plate will vibrate, and the sand will form geometric shapes. Watch the sand grains move around as we play different notes."

First, Jesus played one tone at a time, and each formed a different geometric shape. Then he played ten different tones one right after the other and the sand moved through an ongoing menagerie of shapes.

"Now watch this," he said, clicking a song on his computer. "How about some Rolling Stones!

"You see? You see?" he said, excitedly as the music played. "The sand is jumping around like Mick Jagger on stage."

Then Jesus turned up the volume, tapped his hands on the table, and sang along to the song *Gimme Shelter* – about a storm threatening people's lives – about how war was just a shot away. And the kids, who felt the vibrations, started jumping and dancing to the music. And Jesus continued to sing about how fires and floods were going to cause us all to just fade away – but that there *was* hope, and that *love* was just a kiss away.

When the song ended, the energized children went back and sat on the edge of their seats.

"Wow," said Jesus. "Wasn't that fun?"

"Yeah!" said the kids.

"Well, that's what science can be. I hope you all will consider becoming scientists when you grow up – just like I did."

After making his regular 15-minute climate change presentation to the kids, Jesus opened up the floor to Q&A.

"Is carbon dioxide a greenhouse gas?" asked Cindy.

"Why, yes, it is," replied Jesus, with a broad smile. "And I didn't expect such an adult question from someone so young. I should have known better.

"It is one of six greenhouse gases that affect the atmosphere. The two big ones are carbon dioxide and methane. Methane also comes from fossil fuels and gets into the air mostly from leaks and flares in big gas fields – and from melting permafrost, which is frozen ground in the northern parts of the earth."

"Oh, pop quiz, Mr. Jesus, pop quiz!" said one of the children.

"Okay," said Jesus with a laugh. "Hit me with your best shot."

"What are the other four greenhouse gases."

"Hmmm, that's a tough thing to remember," he replied. "I think they are carbon monoxide, molecular hydrogen, nitrous oxide – and get ready for this one – sulfurhexaflouride."

"Whoa," exclaimed some of the kids, who started applauding."

Any more questions?

"Why can't we just take these greenhouse gases out of the air?" asked another child.

"Actually, a lot of scientists are working on doing exactly that. Removing carbon from the atmosphere on a large scale could very well solve climate change and save the earth. One group has invented a machine that snags CO_2 right out of the air and is trying to turn it into something they can sell such as, fertilizer, or some other useful products. But they still have a lot of work to do.

After taking a few more questions, Jesus changed the subject. "Now, before I go, I'd like to talk to you a little bit about being deaf," he said in a serious tone. "We all know there are five senses: touch, taste, smell, sight, and hearing. Well, did you know that the deaf can see better than the average person?

"That's right. It's because the brain compensates for not being able to hear by increasing the abilities of the other senses. Actually, some deaf people also have better senses of touch, taste, and smell as well as sight. And it's the same for the blind who can hear better than the average person, because their brains compensate for not being able to see.

"Now, from our scientific experiment, we know that we can see sound. Right? So you can be deaf, but you can still hear with your eyes. The Bible says, *'Whoever has eyes to see, let him see.'* Well, I say to you, 'Whoever has eyes to see, let him also hear.'

"Children, I'm asking you not to just see and hear with your eyes, but more than that, to see and hear with your heart. It isn't so hard, especially for the deaf. All you have to do is add a 'T' to the word 'hear,' and you've got 'heart.' H-E-A-R . . . T – HEART. And when all of God's children finally learn to see and hear with our hearts, we become the best we can be.

"Finally, my young friends, I want you to remember that you are the light of world. And I have a gift to remind you of that.

"This is a sound-activated lamp," said Jesus, while pulling it out of his backpack. "All you have to do is plug it in. Now, where should we put it? On the floor or maybe under the table?"

"No," said one of the children. "The Bible says not to put a lamp under a table, because no one can see the light."

"You know your scripture," said Jesus. "We put it up high so it gives light to everyone around."

"Like a city on a hill," said a little girl.

"Just like a city on a hill!" smiled Jesus. "So where should we put it?"

"How about on the credenza?" said the school director. "Is that all right, children?"

Everyone agreed, so Jesus walked over, put the lamp on the credenza, and plugged it in. Then he clapped his hands and the light came on.

Before leaving, Jesus went around to each of the children to say goodbye and they all gave him a big hug.

Arriving early for a meeting at the church, Jesus pulled Rodrigo aside and handed him an envelope full of cash. "Here," he said.

"Global finally gave me my distribution from the matching funds plan and I want you to have it."

"Oh, no," objected Rodrigo, pushing it back. "It is yours. You earned it."

"How long did you work for that company, Rodrigo? Twenty-five years, wasn't it?"

"Si, veinticinco anos."

"And they didn't give you anything when you quit, did they? Not even two weeks severance?"

Rodrigo just looked down and shook his head. "No," he said.

"Well, I think you earned this money more than I did. So here, take it," said Jesus, placing the envelope in his friend's hand.

Then Jesus paused to look around. "Well, most everybody's here," he said. Let's start the meeting."

As the group sat down, Nick strode in and apologized for being late. "Just getting started," said Pete. "Glad you could make it."

"Hey, I have an invitation for Jesus to come back to the office and make a presentation in the auditorium to Global's employees," Nick announced.

"Oh?" said a surprised Jesus.

"Yes, they've noted that you've been skewering the oil and gas industry lately. I think they're offering you an olive branch of sorts."

"I don't know about this," said Pete. "I don't trust those people. It could be dangerous."

"Well, it's true, of course, that an olive branch can yield both good and evil fruit," Jesus replied. "But I believe we have to assume this invitation is sincere."

"I'm not so sure," said Patty. "They're still saying a lot of bad things about you. Lily just never lets up."

"Well, it certainly sounded like the offer was genuine," said Nick. "As for Lily, she's just one bad apple that always flashes a fake smile when she passes me in the hall."

"Did you ever see a tree that was being killed by a vine that covered its trunk?" asked Jesus. "It's very beautiful, but it's like the smiles of certain people. It decorates the ruin it makes."

"Well, that's Lily, for sure," confirmed Aline. "You absolutely cannot trust her. And I believe she is echoing what the executives are saying."

"I know," said Jesus. "They argue that I'm a traitor to the company and to the industry, because they believe the truths we speak are a threat to their way of life, their families, and to how much money they make. But such logic also begs the question: By ignoring the science, by ignoring the facts and the truth, are we not traitors to the human race, to our futures, and to the earth, itself?"

"Of course," agreed Madeleine. "But Jesus, you must accept that some of these people really do hate you."

"Well, I don't hate them," he replied. "In fact, I don't hate anybody. Never really have. And I'd like to think that I left behind something good during my time there. Just like hate is left behind by evil people, love is left behind by good people."

"I still don't think you should go," said Pete. "It'll be hostile. And after all they've done and said about you, they don't deserve your time."

"I agree. Don't go, Jesus."

"Yo no iría allí! I wouldn't go there!" said Rodrigo, emphatically. "No vayas. No te vayas! Don't you go there!"

"My friends, I appreciate your concern. But I'm not afraid of them. Besides, they have already borne false witness against me, slapped me, and fired me. What else can they do to me now?

"Nick, please tell them I accept."

Jesus rose early in the morning so he could drive down to see the sunrise over the lake at Buescher state park. He sat by himself on the shore reading the Bible. When he got to a particular verse, he looked skyward, and spoke it out loud from memory:

"Through the tender mercy of our God, by which the rising sun will come to us from heaven to give light to those that sit in darkness and in the shadow of death, to guide our feet into the way of peace."

The night before, he had told Rodrigo that he was going to visit Austin's school for the blind in the morning and drive back for the presentation at Global's office in the afternoon. "Pete would really like to go with you for at least some level of protection," said Rodrigo.

"No, I will go alone," Jesus replied. "Besides, Nick will be there. He's a good friend, I trust him, and everything will be fine."

He stopped on the way to Austin at Buescher and neighboring Bastrop state parks, because over a four-year period, nearly half of the forests there had been destroyed by wildfires – and he wanted to see the destruction for himself. Tens of thousands of acres had burned, more than 1500 neighboring homes destroyed, and people were seriously injured or killed. Those were only two examples of wildfires that had burned millions of acres in the tall pine forests of Central and East Texas.

Jesus had studied the relationship between climate change and increased wildfires. Rising temperatures, he had learned, cause more droughts and make vegetation drier. Lightning strikes, which happen more frequently in hot weather, or human carelessness can then start forest fires that are often fanned by strong winds driven by climate change. This phenomenon wasn't just happening in Texas, but the world over – in most U.S. states, in several Canadian provinces, and in Spain, Greece, France, and many other countries around the world.

After the sun rose, Jesus spent time walking through the state parks. He saw charred remains of dead trees, some still standing, many laying on the ground, grey ash across the land, burnt soil, erosion from heavy rainfall worsened by the lack of vegetation, evidence of regeneration with fragile new growth, and wildlife searching for food.

After this sojourn, Jesus was off to Austin, less than an hour's drive away.

The grounds of the school for the blind were a blend of old and new buildings, lots of beautifully landscaped wide-open green lawns, and several very large stands of trees surrounding the campus, which seemed like small forests.

Greeting Jesus at the entrance to the main building were the superintendent of the school and two children, who were introduced as Kira and Nazar. "Kira, how very nice to meet you," said Jesus, shaking her extended hand. "Your name has a very ancient history. It means 'beam of light," and may I say it fits you beautifully."

"Thank you," she responded with a wide grin.

"And Nazar, it's my pleasure to meet you, too. Your name was derived from the old country, the Holy Lands, in ancient Christian times. It means 'one who gives.'"

"I didn't know that," he boy responded.

After being escorted inside and setting up his computer presentation, Jesus spoke, as usual, about climate change, running through his slides as if everyone in the room could see them just fine. By the time he got to the Q&A session, hands were popping up all over the room.

"Yes, the young lady with the blonde hair over here."

"That would be you, CeCe," said the superintendent.

"Mr. Jesus, I was reading in this book about planting trees around the world to fight climate change. Do you think that would help?"

Jesus walked over to the girl. "May I see your book, please?" he asked.

"Of course," she said. "Here."

Jesus took the book, which was in braille, ran his hand over the title, and then flipped to a particular page and read it out loud. "'Through photosynthesis, trees absorb carbon dioxide, then release pure oxygen into the atmosphere. So the more trees you plant in the world, the more it helps fight climate change.'

"We must look to all the trees of the field," said Jesus, now talking directly to the girl. "For they are the truth that leads of life. And so you see that the tree of life may very well save the world.

"May I ask how old you are, CeCe?"

"Eleven."

"This is a big book for someone so young," said Jesus. "Do you have an interest in science?"

"Oh, yes, I love science."

"Well, I'm so pleased to hear that. I loved science when I was your age, too. And I hope you'll continue your reading and become a scientist when you grow up.

"Speaking of science," continued Jesus, "I'd like to talk a little about the five senses of touch, taste, smell, hearing, and sight. I'm sure you all know that the blind can hear better than the average person, because the brain compensates for not having the sense of sight by increasing the abilities of the other senses. And many people also have better senses of touch, taste, and smell.

"For instance, I am very sensitive to touch. Have been ever since I can remember. And curiously, you, too, can feel that sensitivity in me. Let me show you."

With that, Jesus walked around to all the children. "Here," he said, "hold my hand long enough for you to feel something."

"Ooooo," came the responses.

"Ahhh."

"I feel it."

"How do you do that?"

"What is it?"

"Well," said Jesus. "I believe it is an energy within me that we can't see or really explain very well. But if others believe, they can also feel it.

"When I was a child," he continued, "my mother asked me to touch my baby sister when her tummy hurt and, almost every time, she stopped crying. Even today, I can sometimes cure small aches and pains when I touch people. But it doesn't always work."

"Can you cure blindness?" asked CeCe.

"Well, in time, science might be able to," said Jesus. "There have already been a lot of advancements, as I'm sure you're aware. Gene therapy, stem cell patches, retinal implants, computer microchips, and so on. Someday, a great scientist will invent a cure for blindness. Maybe, it'll be you, CeCe."

CeCe smiled and blushed slightly.

"Finally, I want to leave something behind for you," said Jesus, pulling a lamp out of his backpack and plugging it in. "This table lamp is a symbol that you, children, are the light of the world. And because most of you can probably hear and feel better than the average person, you have been given a gift, a special talent – and you must use your talents well.

"So I urge you to consider carefully how you listen and how you feel. If you both listen and feel *with your heart*, your whole body will be full of light. Then, just like this lamp, you will give light to all who enter the room. And I promise, if you always listen and feel with your heart, you will one day see the light."

After hanging around with the kids in Austin, Jesus drove back to Houston, returned the car he had borrowed from Father Miguel, and went home for a change of clothes. The day was bright and sunny as he rode his bike over to the office. He waved to many of the shop owners he'd gotten to know on his daily lunch rides when he first joined the company. And he stopped and bought a hot dog from the same local vendor, eating it there as the two chatted away in Spanish.

When he arrived at the building around 3:30 PM, Nick was waiting for him in the lobby. As they greeted each other, the security guard grinned and shouted, "Hey Jesus! You're still not sweating."

"Still cool," replied Jesus, going over to shake the guard's hand.

"Here, let me take your bike and backpack. They'll be right here when you return."

"Thank you, Charles. Good to see you."

Heading toward the main reception area, Nick asked Jesus how he felt coming back and making a presentation.

"Well, you have heard the story, haven't you, about the man as he was ridden out of town on a rail, tarred, and feathered?" Jesus replied. "Somebody asked him how he liked it, and his reply was if it was not for the honor of the thing, he would much rather walk."

Inside the reception area, about ten employees greeted Jesus, including one of the executive vice presidents. "Nice to have you back," he said. "You're message has begun to take hold here. Our employees are filing in for your talk and I think you're going to have a full house."

"Thank you, sir."

Then Nick pulled Jesus aside and told him he was going to head over early. "I want to go over my introduction for you," he said. "Is everything okay? Are you ready?"

"Yes, my heart is ready," said Jesus.

After some more small talk with the people present, everybody but Jesus and Lily had wandered off. "Hello, Jesus," she said. "I'm going to escort you to the auditorium. We'll go through the main hall in administration, where some people are waiting to say hello."

"Okay," he said.

As they reached the same hall Jesus had walked down on his very first day at work, people were standing at their office doors. On the left, the rooms had windows, so it was bright on that side. On the right, there were no windows, and it was more shadowy. Sybil, Bertha, and Mason were on that side, trying to hide behind the door jams so their eyes did not give them away.

Lily stopped at the top of the hallway while Jesus greeted people as he slowly proceeded along. Everyone smiled and some shook his hand as he passed by.

"Hi, Jesus," they said.

"Hello, Jesus."

"Nice to see you, Jesus."

"Welcome back, Jesus."

At the end of the hall, the last man smiled, then lurched forward and violently thrust a knife into Jesus's back.

One woman shrieked in horror. "No!" she screamed. "No!"

Jesus cried out in pain and instinctively turned and grabbed his assailant by the arm. "Jesse!" he said. "My God, Jesse."

Unable to loosen Jesus's grip on his arm, and panicked that he was receiving no support, Jesse yelled out, "Help! Help!"

The others, however, were frozen in place. But then, from the back of the room, Lily, her neck flushed red, her eyes a piercing jet-black, shouted: "Kill him! KILLL HIMMM!"

And then several of those who had just smiled at Jesus, rushed forward and stabbed him in the back. Jesus staggered into the atrium and fell forward toward the painting of the oil company's founder. On the way down he grabbed the linen cloth draped over the table, pulling it and everything else on it to the floor. The stabbing continued while everyone else looked on. Finally, the assailants ran to the back of the hall toward Lily, who led them in a rush out of the building.

Nick, who was standing at the entrance to the auditorium, sprinted over to Jesus, and kneeled down on the bloody floor. "Jesus! Jesus!," he cried out. "My God! My God!"

Hearing Nick's voice, Jesus raised his head and turned left where there was a sunbeam shining through the window. "Look," he murmured, "a certain slant of light."

Then Jesus dropped his head and his voice tapered to a whisper. Nick leaned down and heard him say, "Heavenly hurt it gives us."

"Jesus," said Nick, softly, "Stay with us."

Jesus moved his lips and said something only Nick could possibly have heard. Then he lost consciousness. A security guard who had rushed to the scene knelt down, checked for a pulse, and announced that Jesus was gone.

Nick stood up and others crowded around in stunned silence.

They saw Jesus laying in a pool of blood clutching the crimson stained Byssus linen.

And the flame on the last candle burning flickered out.

The five top company executives sat in their president's study smoking Cuban cigars and drinking the best Scotch money could buy.

"Well, men, time to celebrate," said Curtis. "We took care of that S.O.B."

"We sure did. And good riddance."

"You know, it was a lot easier than I thought it would be," said Curtis. "I guess when you have an unlimited supply of money and are working with idiots, anything is possible."

"Yeah, Lily. What a stupid bitch."

"Should we go to the funeral?"

"The kid's funeral? Absolutely not."

"No, I meant Lily's."

"Oh, we might make an appearance."

"I don't know, Curtis – after all, she *is* the villain in all this," said one of the VPs with a wry look on his face."

The men all laughed and hoisted their glasses in a toast. Just then there was a knock on the study door.

"Yes, come in," said the boss.

It was the butler. "Excuse me, sir," he said. "The TV says the eye of the hurricane will pass right over us. Major flooding is forecast. Looks like it's going to be quite bad, sir."

Curtis shot to his feet and started barking out orders. "Instruct the staff to put the cover on the swimming pool. Pull my Porsche into the garage. Get the furniture out of the gazebo. Move all the art to the second floor. You know what else to do. Move! Move! Move! Let's go! Let's go!"

The other executives put down their drinks and rushed to their cars. The celebration was over.

Our Lady of Guadalupe church was filled that afternoon. People had begun arriving more than an hour early. They filled the pews, stood around the walls inside, and waited quietly on the grounds outside. There were local residents from the neighborhood and employees from the oil and gas industry, including many from Global Energy. All the members of Jesus's close group were there, including the geologists, geophysicists, engineers, and the geochemist. Others present were local scientists, ladies of the evening, downtown shop owners, the hot dog vendor, and Charles, the security guard, who had placed Jesus's bike and backpack in front of the first row of pews.

When the simple wooden casket was brought in, there was a hushed silence – broken only by weeping. Pete, Nick, Rodrigo, Father Miguel, Juan, and a homeless man were the pallbearers. Father Miguel placed an open Bible and crucifix on the casket. Then he moved to the altar. The pallbearers took seats on the front pew next to Madeleine, Patty, and Aline who tried to comfort the deeply despondent Nick and Rodrigo.

The service began with opening prayers, music and Biblical readings. Then the Deacon spoke:

"A reading from the Gospel according to Matthew:

All the nations will be assembled before him. And he will separate them one from another . . . .

Then [He] will say to those on his right . . . "Come, you who are blessed by my father. Inherit the kingdom prepared for you from the foundation of the world. For I was hungry and you gave me food, I was thirsty and you gave me drink, a stranger and you welcomed me, naked and you clothed me, ill and you cared for me, in prison and you visited me."

Then the righteous will answer him and say, "Lord, when did we see you hungry and feed you, or thirsty and give you drink, . . . a stranger and welcome you . . . naked and clothe you . . . ill or in prison and visit you?"

"Whatever you did for one of these least brothers of mine, you did for me.'

Then he will say to those on the left . . . "Depart from me . . . into the eternal fire prepared for the devil and his angels." For I was hungry and you gave me no food, thirsty and you gave me no drink, a stranger and you gave me no welcome, naked and you gave me no clothing, ill and in prison and you did not care for me."

Then they will answer and say, "Lord, when did we see you hungry or thirsty or a stranger or naked or ill or in prison, and not minister to your needs?"

"What you did not do for one of these least ones, you did not do for me."

And these will go off to eternal punishment, but the righteous to eternal life.

"The Gospel of the Lord."

"Praise to you, Lord Jesus Christ," the congregation responded.

Father Miguel then stepped forward to deliver the homily.

"Thank you all for attending," he began. "I admire the many people from around town who braved the elements to be here. I'm not sure how the word got out during the storm. We were expecting a small crowd.

"We give thanks that this storm did not linger but moved through rapidly. It was a Category 5 hurricane, even stronger than the last one. And it seems to have spared our church and most of our neighborhood. I don't know why, but it seems that most of the rest of the city is in serious trouble – as is much of our nation. And we pray for the many victims of this storm, and for our brothers and sisters in California and Colorado who are fighting recent outbreaks of forest fires and flooding.

"The bad weather is one reason that our friend's immediate family is not here. But there will be another service and then burial in California."

Father Miguel paused for a few moments, took a deep breath, and softly said:

"Jesus Garcia Gomez."

"He once told me that, to him, the Gospel we just heard, from Matthew, *The Judgment of the Nations,* was one of the most important passages in the New Testament. And, indeed, he lived the guidance in that passage. He served food to the hungry, built homes for those in need, and did many things for many people who will forever remain unknown to most of us. But in our church today are some we do know about.

"There are people here from East Texas who were surprised when Jesus showed up the weekend after a tornado damaged their homes. He gave them cash, hired local contractors to help rebuild, and stayed to work with them through the weekend.

"There is a woman here, Mrs. Romero, who has revealed that Jesus cured her arthritis simply by holding her hands in his.

"And there is a woman whose child was saved by Jesus. During the last storm, he dashed out to their submerged car, pulled her out, got her back to shore, and revived her by giving mouth-to-mouth resuscitation. The mother and daughter are both here today – as are so many friends of Jesus. Indeed, he was a friend to everybody with whom he came into contact.

"Jesus lived the word of the Lord as well as anyone I've ever met," continued Father Miguel. "He was particularly fond of saying that God's first instruction to humanity was to 'serve and protect' the earth and to 'till and keep it.' So I feel I would be particularly remiss if I did not restate his firm belief that climate change is real and that we human beings are causing it. There is a certain foreboding in this most recent storm, because he warned us about the increased probability of such events. Of course, history will judge whether his scientific conclusions and predictions will come true.

"One of Jesus's most important legacies in his short time here on earth, I believe, is that he worked diligently to bridge the gap between religion and science. 'They can coexist,' he said. 'They must coexist.' 'Science,'" he once told me, 'is a human being's way of understanding the truth and beauty of God's universe.'

"I believe we must heed his advice and do all we can to reverse the course we seem to be on. Jesus left us knowing we have a choice. We can either sit still – or we can take action to save the earth and the people living on it. Will the movement he led die with him or will it live on?

"It's up to us."

Father Miguel took another long pause. Then a wisp of a smile crossed his face.

"And finally, before we offer communion, I'd like to take a moment to explain the hand gesture that Jesus always used. Most people think of it as Mr. Spock's "Vulcan Salute" from Star Trek, after which he usually said: 'Live long and prosper.'

"But did you know that this sign is Biblical in origin? Deuteronomy includes the phrase 'live and prosper' as part of what Moses said to the Hebrew people entering Canaan. Numbers reads: 'The Lord bless thee and keep thee.' And the Gospel of John says, 'I have come so that they may have life, and may have it abundantly.'

"You see then, that the gesture Jesus used when he waved goodbye is, in fact, an ancient Jewish blessing for eternal life. So, in a tribute to our most beloved friend, I ask you all today to please hold up your hand like this, and on the count of three, we will all say out loud and to each other, 'Live long and prosper.' Go ahead, raise your hands."

As the crowd held up their hands, most were having a bit of trouble making the gesture.

"I know, I know," said Father Miguel with a smile, "it's kind of hard to keep the pinky and ring fingers together. So you can use your other hand to bring them together. Adults help the children – or, perhaps, more appropriately, children help the adults."

Soon there was giggling and laughing as everybody tried to help each other get the sign right. Finally, all had a hand up and the church became quiet.

"Okay, ready?" asked Father Miguel. "One, two, three . . . "

. . . and the people all said: "LIVE LONG AND PROSPER."

That evening, the closest friends of Jesus got together in a separate room of the church. Nick was still inconsolable. "I feel like I betrayed him," he said. "I'm the one who invited him there. I thought it would be okay. My God, I'm a Judas. How could I have been so stupid?"

"You are no Judas, Nick," said Pete. "You're a good man."

"Si," agreed Rodrigo. "Tu no eres Judas. But Jesse! No entiendo. Jesus was kind to him. Even gave his own bike when Jesse's was stolen."

"How could it be that, in Jesse's mind, he went from being good to so bad to the point where he would actually murder Jesus?" asked Nick. "I don't understand, either."

"I do," said Patty. "It was Lily. She must have worked her evil on him. She knew Jesse was easily influenced – and those are the kind of people she preyed upon."

"Somebody said she screamed 'Kill him!' and then the others rushed up to help Jesse stab him."

"They all have said Lily was the mastermind."

"Well, we'll never know now, will we?" said Nick.

"What do you mean?"

"You mean you haven't heard?"

"Heard what?"

"Lily was run over by a car last night. She's dead."

For a few moments, there was a stunned silence.

"Well, she was definitely one of the leaders," said Pete. "But I'm not sure if there were others. Who issued the invitation, Nick? Was it Lily?"

"No, it was Curtis, the president of the company."

Another silent pause. Then Father Miguel changed the subject. "Jesus was the most Christian person I ever met," he said. "I can't imagine him being better if he was the second coming."

"Maybe a few miracles," said Aline.

"What about those two ladies?" asked Madeleine. "He cured one with arthritis and saved the other's little girl."

"Jesus always downplayed things like that as some sort of magnetic field in his hands," said Pete. "He said it only worked for small things and sometimes it didn't work at all."

"Well, he did have an eerie human excellence, didn't he?

"Yes, he did."

"Hey, Nick, would you mind telling us what Jesus said just before he died?" asked Patty.

"Well, he turned his head toward the sunbeam shining through the window and said, "Look, a certain slant of light . . . . Heavenly hurt."

"What does that mean?"

"I'm not sure."

Then Nick's voice started to break. "And Jesus finally whispered, just before he lost consciousness, . . . he whispered 'Forgive them.'"

There was a very long silence as emotions swept through the group.

"Those were his last words?" asked Father Miguel.

With tears rolling down his face, Nick nodded yes.

After another few moments, Madeleine broke the silence. "I didn't know his last name was Gomez," she said. "I thought it was Garcia."

"It was both," noted Rodrigo. "First name derived from the father. Second name from the mother. Es tradicion."

"You mean Gomez was his mother's name?"

"Si."

"And you know the meaning of Gomez, don't you?" asked Father Miguel.

Everybody looked at the priest.

"It means 'Son of Man.'"

Early the next morning in the children's cancer hospital ward, a child ran past the nurse's station. Then another. Then another. And before you knew it, dozens of children were running up and down the halls – some in circles, some with airplane arms extended.

"What in the world?" asked the head nurse to nobody in particular.

"It's as if they had been cooped up on long family trip and have just been let out of the car!" exclaimed another nurse.

Pretty soon all of the children were up and moving about. Some went to the big room and started playing games with each other. The nurses on duty spread out, walked down the halls, and peered into the rooms. They saw kids jumping up and down on their beds. One little boy was yelling, "I'm hungry! I'm hungry!" A little girl popped her head out from behind a chair and said, "Peekaboo!" Then she giggled and dashed out of the room. Another child running down the hall, stopped to tap a nurse on the arm, and said: "You're it!" Then he took off again.

The head nurse finally called the doctor on duty. "You better get up here, immediately," she said. "Kids are going crazy."

"Which ones?" he asked.

"All of them! Hurry."

The doctor shot up the stairs as fast as he could. When he opened the stairwell door, several children ran into him. Then he walked down the hall in disbelief at what was happening.

"What do you think, Doctor?" the head nurse asked.

"Well, these kids certainly don't look sick to me," he replied.

"What should we do? Should we try to corral them and calm them down?"

"I don't think so. Let them run."

"Have you ever seen anything like this?"

"No, never. We better call all their physicians in right away for examinations."

"Okay," said the nurse. "We're on it."

"Let's call their parents, too," said the doctor. "This is unbelievable."

Early this same morning, Cindy, the little red-haired girl at the local school for the deaf, slowly got out of bed, walked into the hall, and then down to the atrium. It was still dark, very quiet, and Cindy, as she had a tendency to do, was sleepwalking.

She walked over toward the lamp on the credenza and stood in front of it for several moments. Then she clapped her hands. The lamp came on and Cindy suddenly woke up. She saw the light, looked around, realized that she was sleepwalking again, and decided to go back to bed. So she clapped her hands together to turn off the lamp – and it startled her.

"What was that?" she thought to herself.

She clapped her hands, again, the light came on – and she was startled again. "Oooo," she muttered out loud.

Then she began clapping her hands over and over again and the light kept going on and off. "Ooooo! Oooooo! Ooooooooo!" said Cindy louder and louder each time.

Now jumping up and down, Cindy, raced to the center of the atrium, ran around in circles, and just screamed as loud as she could.

Lights started coming on around the school. As the children woke up, they headed toward the atrium, went up to Cindy – and they, too, began screaming.

After a few minutes, the night teacher on duty came out of her room and went to the atrium. "What in the world is going on?" she said in sign language. But nobody paid any attention to her. The kids just kept yelling and hugging each other. So she walked into the crowd of kids and touched Cindy on the shoulder. "What's going on," she again signed.

The girl jumped into her teacher's arms and hugged her.

"Calm down, Cindy," signed the teacher. "What's going on?"

"Oh, Miss Amy," Cindy signed back. "We can hear. We can all hear!!'

"What?" said Amy. "What? That can't be! How can that be?"

And outside, the sun slowly rose over the horizon.

That same morning in Austin's school for the blind, CeCe, who slept near a window, woke up at the crack of dawn – well before her alarm clock sounded. She seemed to see a blurred off-white color. So she rubbed her eyes, closed them, and opened them again. Then she turned and looked toward the window, squinting at the day's first light.

CeCe then got up, walked to the bathroom, looked in the mirror, and saw her face for the very first time. She touched her cheek, her lips, her forehead. She turned the water on, splashed her face and dried it, pausing to look in wonder at the towel. Then she looked back in the mirror at herself – and began to cry.

CeCe next walked down the hall toward the large gathering room, closing her eyes so she could navigate as she'd done a thousand times before. When she got to the room, she walked to the lamp Jesus had left behind. She reached over, flicked the switch, and when the light came on, it startled her. She just stood there for the longest time staring at that lamp.

Soon, Nazar walked in and stood next to her. Then Kira. And then more and more children until there were about ten kids silently looking at the lamp on the table.

"Can the rest of you see, too?" asked Nazar, breaking the silence.

"Yes, I think so."

"Yes, me too."

"And me."

Then the kids began looking at each other, touching faces, and talking. Soon they recognized voices and saw their friends for the first time. Then the tears came. Then the shouting and screaming for joy. Then all the school children got out of bed and wandered into the room.

And they could all see.

After a few minutes, Kira and CeCe, who were the best of friends, walked hand in hand toward the big window that faced out back. They wanted to take a look outside. CeCe had gone blind at the age of seven. Kira had been born blind.

"Kira, look at the different colors," said CeCe. "Aren't they beautiful?"

"I can't tell what the colors are," replied Kira. "I've never seen them before.'

CeCe then began to point. "Look," she said, "the sky is blue. The clouds are white. The grass is green. And the trees over there are green, too, just darker green."

"Oh, look," continued CeCe. "There's a man."

"A man? Where?" asked Kira.

"Right over there in front of the trees. He has a bicycle with him and a backpack slung over his shoulder. Do you see him?"

"Yes, I think I do."

"He sees us. He's holding up his hand. Oh, he's waving to us. Quick, let's wave back."

As the two girls waved, the man smiled.

Then he turned and walked into the woods.

But he left his bike behind.

ABOUT THE AUTHOR

DONALD T. PHILLIPS is a *New York Times* best-selling author. His book, *Lincoln On Leadership*, helped pave the way toward the creation of a new genre of books on historical leadership. He holds Bachelors and Masters degrees in geology, and has been studying climate change for the past thirty years.

Made in the USA
Columbia, SC
27 August 2019